Colpetty People

Stories

Perera - Hussein Publishing House

Ashok Ferrey

Colpetty People

Stories

Ph
Perera - Hussein Publishing House

Published by the Perera-Hussein Publishing House, 2005
ISBN 955-8897-01-9

Third print 2005

Printed and bound in Sri Lanka by Piyasiri Printing Systems
Typeset by The Fontmaster
Cover design by Muhannad Cader
Photograph of couch by Dominic Sansoni
Illustrations by Ashok Ferrey

Contents

For Amantha Helena

and to the memory of

St. Clair Sylvester George

The Perfect House

I had always wanted to build the perfect house. For years I had looked at other people's, surreptitiously, because as you know, houses don't like to be stared at, whatever their owners might think. It had to be small, it had to be in the city. Not for me those dreaming palaces tucked away in the golden countryside: that too was a beautiful dream, but it was not my dream. All I knew was that my house had to have a window on either side of the entrance, widely spaced like the eyes of a beautiful woman, and that you would be able to look straight through from the front to the back. That was all. I need hardly add that I had never built a house before.

Well, it all happened, and it took longer and was more painful than childbirth. (I can hear the wife snorting in the kitchen.) Of course once I had built it, I couldn't afford to live in it, the interest payments on the loan being so high. So I tried to give it out on rent, and then nobody wanted to rent it either. Trouble was, you see, it didn't look like a house. Some people said it looked like a church, other people said it looked like a casino. It had three floors.

"How do you manage to get to the bedrooms?" they asked.

"With the agility of a mountain goat," I replied.

A famously budding restaurateur wanted it, to start a swine-dining establishment. "I must have it," he said, "just bear with me till I give notice at my present place." That was eleven years ago, and I am still waiting, Henry.

Then along came Ulla, the answer to all my prayers. She arrived in an ancient silver Bentley, tall and blonde and very beautiful (Ulla, not the Bentley). I wondered idly how the house would take to her. Ulla was a big girl: you looked at her and you thought Wagner, the Ring Cycle, and all those flaxen maidens rushing back and forth across the stage in golden horns, shrieking and bellowing.

"Why is it," she asked, "every house in Colombo has its garage opening into the sitting room?"

I laughed loudly because mine didn't, the garage being tucked away in the basement.

"I like it," she bellowed, "I'll take it."

Now the house is built in a cunning way, to look much larger than it actually is. You have to be very clever about what you put in it. Once Ulla entered the sitting room there was room for little else, so my heart sank when all this curly-wurly repro furniture started to arrive.

Mine not to reason why, I thought sadly. It's as if you've just given away your beautiful daughter at the altar to a man who, you discover too late, wears gold chains round his neck and grows the nail on his little finger long.

I left her to it and, really, the first year was fine because Ulla had paid the year's rent in advance on signing the lease. How little I knew then about the gentle art of landlordism in Sri Lanka. Ulla had two teenage daughters, Helga and Hannah - not half as lovely as the mother - and two servants, an old boy called Odiris, and a half-wit called Thomas who had fallen from a coconut tree when he was young and was a bit desiccated as a result.

When the second year's rent was due, I gave it a week out of tact, and another out of delicacy, then I went round.

Odiris was standing at the basement entrance smoking a vile local cheroot. Thomas was with him, looking, well, vacant.

"*Hamu né*," said Thomas. My lady isn't in. Odiris said nothing, but pointed upwards silently with the smoking cheroot: for this little gesture I have loved him like a brother ever since. Hamu was obviously in, but not at home to the likes of me.

I went in and sat down on a satinwood repro, directly under what I knew was Ulla's bedroom. Now I built this house from the odds and sods they were throwing out when they demolished the old UNP headquarters at Sri Kotha. The recycled teak floors I had installed upstairs were a dead giveaway. A creak here, a creak there: I could imagine Ulla gliding about up there, noiselessly as she fondly imagined. I dug myself in and read *The Island* paper from cover to cover, all three pages of it. Then I had a brainwave.

"Tell Hamu I'll be back another day," I shouted from the verandah to the two domestics. I slammed the door shut, and silently sat down again. Five minutes passed. Then an almighty bellow:

"Thomas! Has he gone yet?" Ulla was halfway down the double-return staircase before she noticed me, sitting there quietly, like a mouse among its droppings.

"Ashok," she said, switching on a smile like a long-life bulb, "you've caught me at a bad time, you naughty boy! Why didn't you call before you came?" (Because you would *definitely* have made sure you were out then).

"I don't have anything for you at the moment, but why don't you try me next week?" (Yes dear, that too, but what about my rent?)

"I'll come on Tuesday," I replied.

On Tuesday she came downstairs with a box.

"No rent, I'm afraid, but this is a present from me to you." It was a puppy, and we named him Pooch. Life is *such* a bitch.

Another week went by and nothing happened. You may ask why I didn't send round a thundering letter of demand through a lawyer. The simple answer is that Sri Lankan lawyers are not what they are meant to be, and in a second Ulla would have had the demanding lawyer eating out of her hand, or on her lap, or both, and my case would have been out the window.

"Let's invite her to the little fellow's birthday party," suggested the wife. (She can be quite clever at times, the little homemaker.)

Now these Sri Lankan parties are not your western style crisp-and-twiglet affairs. There are jugglers and magic shows and pony rides. And that's just for the adults.

Ulla made a big entrance in a small skirt, and immediately gathered together a following of young fathers. They trailed her round and round the garden hoping she would reveal a little of her German magic. Really, I needn't have bothered with the ponies.

A couple of hours later, when the young fathers were beginning to thin out, I tracked Ulla down to a stone bench in the garden.

"These are very good," she said, knocking back an arrack and passion fruit cocktail. "This is my fourth."

"Ulla," I began.

"I know what you're going to say," she interrupted, fishing about absently in a large tapestry bag. She pulled out a brown envelope. "I didn't get your boy a birthday present because I knew you'd prefer this."

There was ten thousand in the envelope, a long way short of the rent.

"Ashok, Ashok, if only you knew how difficult life is for me..." she crossed and recrossed her legs to show just how difficult. "...I have to find dowries for Hanna and Helga..."

Dowries! I thought to myself, these amazing white women, they come out to live in Sri Lanka and become more Sri Lankan than us natives. They treat us like shit, and God how we love it! It's a sort of new age colonialism, but with very willing subjects. I took the money humbly, gratefully, thankfully. I would have doffed my cap if I'd had one.

◼ ◼ ◼

In the course of the year I must have gone to the house at least twenty times, coming away each time with two thousand here, three thousand there. Once when I arrived she was defrosting her fridge, passing out stuff to Helga and Hanna.

"You have no idea how hard it is for us business people," she said sternly. A selection of hams and salamis was beginning to emerge from the fridge.

"Things are *so* depressed." Smoked pork knuckles from Keells.

"I don't know *how* I'm going to manage if things get any worse." Bottles and bottles of chilled Liebfraumilch.

"You should have got her to pay you in knuckles," said the wife wistfully when I came home empty-handed.

Worst of all, the house, my beloved house, was beginning to show the strain. Two beautiful women can never really coexist satisfactorily under the one roof without one or other giving way: there was damp in the basement and white ants in the walls. Thomas and Odiris were never allowed upstairs unless Ulla was present · did she have money stashed under the mattress? - and she hardly ever was.

As a result the cleaning and tidying hardly ever got done, the doors and windows never opened. Any clothes to be washed were thrown casually over the balustrade from upstairs to the sitting room below. I know, because I was at the receiving end once. (Don't ask).

Another time I went to the house I was greeted by the words "*Hamu ispiritale*" My lady's in hospital.

Ulla was ensconced in a double-aspect corner room at the New World Hospital, suffering from an allergy. You have to be an expert string-puller to get one of these rooms, which are usually booked months in advance and cost as much per day as a labourer gets in a month. She was attended by a coterie of minions, Miss Balthazar who operated the fax, Sanju the office boy, and various smartly dressed gents.

"Ashok," she said, "how good of you to come." I composed my features into a 'concerned' look.

"Look!" she said whipping back the sheets. (Miss Balthazar averted her eyes). The famous legs had swelled and turned a delicious pale crimson, like two smoked hams from Keells.

"But I haven't forgotten any of you." She looked magnanimously at me and the natty gents. As if on cue Miss Balthazar stepped forward under the weight of an enormous cheque-book. Ulla signed and presented me with not one, but three cheques.

"This for now, this a week later, and this a week after that." Triple the pleasure. The natty gents received one each.

"You can cash them at my bank in Fort." She leant back to show that the audience was at an end. I shared a three-wheeler into Fort with my fellow creditors. At the bank entrance there was a bit of a scuffle. I had paid for the taxi so they were politely insisting I go in first.

"Age before beauty," I said and rolled in. And so it happened that my cheque got presented first, and was the only one that was realised, there being insufficient funds for theirs. I came away a happy man: it doesn't pay to be too polite in Colombo these days.

Of course there is a footnote, a postscript to this tale. My two other cheques, duly presented a week and fortnight later, both bounced. I now find that this seems to be standard Sri Lankan business practice, so I can hardly blame Ulla too much.

"She'll have to go," said the wife, and I agreed sadly; but it was the house that took the initiative in the final *putsch*, the putting in of the boot. Late one rainy night the following week I got a frantic call. "Come immediately!"

I drove over to the house in the pelting rain.

Ulla was standing in a pool of water, and for a moment there I thought she had lost all control.

"Just look at this house!" She began to shriek and bellow, a Wagnerian counterpoint to the raging storm outside. "Riddled with termites, and now this bloody leaking roof!"

"You're right," I agreed calmly. "It's best if you try to find another house. I will, of course, refund any rent that has been overpaid." This was a joke because it was actually she who was owing me rent. But she brightened up considerably at this and we parted almost friends.

Weeks passed and there was no sign of her moving. Paying the rent was obviously out of the question now she had decided to go, and I did not press her for fear she might change her mind and stay. It was October once again, and the Oberoi Hotel was having its usual Oktoberfest celebration. I remember it well because at our table that year we had the actor Julian Sands who had flown over to film something out here. Ulla sailed past, a silly party hat on her head, in the arms of the German Ambassador.

"I have an idea," I said to the wife, as we silently consumed our pickled pig's knuckles and boiled potatoes.

She gave a loud snort, but then she is given to snorting, or possibly it was the presence of so much pig around.

Next day I went over in the afternoon, having given Ulla time to sober up. She wasn't there, but Helga was, the nicer of the two daughters.

"You know," I said, "the German Ambassador is a very close friend of my mother's." (The Gentle Art of Landlordism, Chapter Two: Bullshitting with Finesse.) "I would hate for him to find out that Ulla is having trouble paying the rent. Colombo is *such* a small place."

Within a week she was gone, with three months rent owing, but did I care? There was also an unpaid telephone bill of 165,000 rupees. And the really amazing thing, the phone was still on: us poor natives get cut off for a mere fifteen thousand. I can just imagine her, big and blonde, at Sri Lanka Telecom:

"Life is *so* hard. I have to find dowries for two daughters..."

◉ ◉ ◉

As you probably know, my beloved house is now the Café Xenon, with grey walls and scarlet columns. Instead of the dowdy Oxfam clothes she once wore, the beautiful woman is now in permanent evening dress. I must confess it is not entirely to my taste. In the harsh light of the tropical day, she sometimes looks like a drunken party guest who has gone to sleep and woken up in the clothes of the night before. But I realise that she will be around long after you and I are dead and gone, houses being more immortal than us mere humans, and maybe someone, somewhere down the line, will restore her to her once pristine beauty.

Ô Signore, Non Sono Degno

Thump, thump, thump, the beat of the drum floated across the African savannah.

"What's that?" asked Romesh, "a talking drum?" The famous talking drum of West Africa was used to send messages from one village to another.

"That's the music from the Costain Club." Ogun Brown gave him a bemused look. "Have you never been there?"

Romesh shook his head. "Now put your books away everybody," he called out loudly, "lights out." He closed the dormitory door, realising that was the signal for the fun to begin: the students were only waiting for him to leave. It's not my problem, he thought to himself as he walked out. The school lay in open ground, serenaded by the sounds of the Costain Club like sweet music from a distant oasis. Romesh walked past the classroom block, the silent chapel and the empty guard-house. Home was only five minutes away. His thoughts went back to a month ago, when it all began...

"Telegram for you, Romesh," his mother sang out from the bottom of the stairs. Romesh was having a late, late lie-in. It was 8.14 in the morning. She did not usually let him get beyond 7.59 but today was Christmas Eve.

Romesh's mother opened the telegram and read out the contents for him to hear. She opened all his mail. "Congratulations place Christ Church regards Father Dominic"

Romesh heaved a sigh of relief. Oxford here I come, he thought as he rolled over, putting the pillow on his head. But not for long. Mrs. Silva swept in, throwing open the windows and drawing the curtains. She liked to get the rooms all done before nine, so that it left her day free. There was a houseboy or 'steward' who came in to help her once a week. His name was Sunday but he usually came on Monday.

Not that there was that much to do with her free time out here. 'Out here' was Kaduna, capital of the North Central State of Nigeria, hardly changed from the colonial backwater it had been in the days before independence. In her free time Mrs. Silva played bridge and made marmalade, though not at the same time. She had tried once, but the burning smell from the kitchen made her trump her partner's ace, and her partner did not speak to her for a month. If bridge was serious business in Kaduna so was marmalade: hers was so popular she even supplied the Hamdala, Kaduna's only hotel.

Oxford would begin the following October, nine months away.

"We'll fix you up with a teaching job at St. John's in the meantime," said Mr. Silva when he came home from work. They had it all planned out for him: the teaching job, the Oxford degree, the nine-to-five forever and ever after, Amen. It was the way of the East: Romesh was seventeen but he might as well have been seven. Back home in Sri Lanka there were men of thirty who were afraid to marry because their mother wouldn't like it. Romesh even had an elderly cousin in his fifties who had to ask permission before he took the car out of the garage.

"And you can even have the car." It was as if they were reading his mind. "It's not safe for a child to be walking on these streets. There was another kidnapping yesterday. I heard about it at the Ministry." Romesh's father was financial controller at the Ministry of Finance, the fount of all wisdom as far as he was concerned. God give me strength, Romesh prayed silently. St. John's College was only two streets away, a mission school before the state took it over. There were still priests, Italians, and even the odd nun, but they stayed very much in the background and the teaching was mostly by lay staff. The school was run by a Pakistani couple, the Shaqs, or Sharks as they were popularly known. It was said that Mr. Shaq had been a bicycle mechanic in Cawnpore before partition. Mrs. Shaq was Head of English, and her English was atrocious.

Romesh went for the interview in his one and only Harrods school suit. The job was a foregone conclusion but appearances had to be kept up. Mrs. Shaq conducted the interview, a superbly sleek woman with oiled hair and powdered skin. She wore rings on her fingers and quite probably bells on her toes. She played hard to get, shuffling around the papers on her desk for a long time. Finally she looked up, favouring him with a pearly smile.

"You're in luck," said Mrs. Shaq.

Romesh taught Maths and English for O' Level. His classes had over fifty children, a fair number of whom were older than him. One week out of every four Romesh was duty master, which meant turning the lights out at 9.15 in the evening. Discipline was virtually non-existent, and teaching wasn't easy given the wide range of ages and intellectual abilities, but there were some brilliant students, one of whom was Ogun Brown.

"You really should be using the car," said his mother when he got home that night.

"But it's only two streets away."

"I don't want my baby getting kidnapped."

Romesh shuddered and went upstairs. He longed for the holidays, for his friends to arrive. Like a swarm of locusts the expat children, mostly English, would fly in for the school holidays. There were twenty or thirty of them, a screeching host that laid waste to the town and upset the residents. They were above the law, being the sons and daughters of the local police chief, the doctor, the bank manager and so on. The year before, two of them had knocked down and killed a pedestrian, coming back from a night club in the early hours. The case had not even reached the newspapers let alone the courts.

Romesh's best friend Jack was the son of the chief engineer at the Ministry of Works, a dour Scotsman who it was rumoured beat his wife. Jack's mother in turn found her consolation in the bottle, and was never without her gin and tonic from early morning. They lived in a half-timbered mock Tudor mansion in the middle of a jungle clearing. Kaduna was mostly like that: little pockets of civilization set in the ever-encroaching scrub wilderness.

"You're the son of that Indian chappie," she said to him in one of her rare moments of lucidity.

"Not Indian," he corrected gently, "Sri Lankan." She smiled helplessly, as if to say, "Well, it may matter to you, young man, but how can it possibly matter to me?"

Jack hurried him away. Contact between his parents and friends was kept to a bare minimum. Even though they had their own swimming pool, Romesh and the others were hardly ever invited round. Instead, everyone congregated at the Hamdala Hotel pool: they could quite as easily have met at the Kaduna Club or the Crocodile Club or the Polo Club - oh how these English loved their clubs! - but the Hamdala pool was headquarters. There was only one problem: membership was expensive.

Romesh was paid seventy naira a month, a pittance even then in the Seventies. They were fortunate to have him at St. John's, he thought, a budding Oxford graduate. *You don't know your luck, Mrs. Shaq.*

"Now that you're earning good money," said his mother, "you can pay for your few extras."

'Few extras!' he thought with despair. The weekly cinema ticket at the Kaduna Club, the drinks (brandy-ginger or Star beer), the entry to La Cabana (the only *decent* night club). The monthly pool ticket alone was thirty naira.

"But of course we'll pay for the petrol in the car," she added. This was hardly as generous as it sounded. Nigeria in its oil-producing heyday was awash with petrol: it was actually cheaper than bottled water. Even the Shaqs, those notorious skinflints, drove around in a powder-blue Chevrolet Impala the size of a small bungalow, that did about two gallons to the mile.

Work was exhausting. There is nothing like teaching to make you realise that you will never be a good teacher. He was one of the lucky ones, with only a nine month sentence, and then Oxford and freedom. But there were lifers, like Sister Raphael the history teacher, and of course the Shaqs, and he wondered how they managed. There were days when he would have gladly lined his students up against a wall and machine-gunned the lot. At six every evening there was Italian mass in the chapel said by the mission priests. It was the high point of Romesh's day, standing at the back in the gloom with the ebb and flow of the voices around him. It was like being at a foreign film or at the opera: you heard the

sounds and you knew their sense even if you didn't know
their exact meaning. His favourite was the bit when they
chanted:

"*Ô Signore, non sono degno di partecipare alla tua
mensa, ma di soltanto la parola e io saro salvato.*" O Lord, I
am not worthy to receive you, but only say the word and I
shall be healed.

The words were like waves breaking on the distant
shore of a foreign land, twice as beautiful in Italian as in
English. And when mass was over, the sky outside was a
deep pink like the inside of a giant shell, the grand opera of
an African sunset that lasted five minutes only, before the
curtain fell.

◊ ◊ ◊

It was financial desperation that drove him to Sindy
Adobanele, or so Romesh liked to think afterwards. She was
the girl who sold the tickets at the Hamdala pool.

"Is that your car?" she asked pointing to his father's
metallic green Opel.

"Sometimes." She had buttery skin and her long
fingernails were cut square at the ends.

"I wish I could drive." It wasn't a hint, more a wistful
comment like, 'I wish I were taller.'

"Would you like me to teach you?" he asked quickly.

"How can you, if it's not your car?"

"It's my father's. He lets me use it in the afternoons.
Look, when you finish up here I could take you for a round
if you like."

"I finish my shift at five," she said. She didn't charge him for his ticket.

On the first day they didn't go very far. Kaduna was small enough that after ten minutes of driving you were more or less out in open country. He took her past the school and round the savannah, and past the Costain Club. When he taught her to change gears his hand stayed on hers and she didn't seem to mind.

"Can I drop you home?" he asked.

"It's OK," she said quickly, "you can take me back to the hotel."

He left her there and went to mass, and the waves of sound washed over his inert body and gave his mind the release it craved.

The next day she allowed him to take her home after the lesson. She lived right in the center of town, next to Iossofidis, the Greek department store, above a clothes shop.

"I guess you're busy," she started to say, but he cut in,

"I'd like to come in, if I may."

They went up the narrow linoleum-lined staircase, to her iron door.

"Home," she said in a flat voice.

There was a largish room to the front overlooking the road and a small kitchen at the back, with a balcony over the yard of the shop below. A curtain of red glass beads separated the two. Off the kitchen, strangely, was a small w.c. That was it.

"I wash in the kitchen sink," she explained reading his thoughts. "And I have my showers at the pool."

His eyes took in the dark brown walls, the divan with its bedspread of densely-woven stripes, and the curious red light filtering through the glass beads. Chocolate and ruby and lime: the colours of West Africa.

When he was very young, three or four at most, someone had given him a rosary of red plastic beads. Romesh could still remember sitting in his baby bath, looking through a bead at the cruel red world outside. It gave him a feeling of melancholy and discontent, of despair almost, for the journey that lay ahead, the trials that had to be faced in an adult world. He wanted to turn back, stop the clocks, pull the bedclothes over his head, but at the same time he knew with a sinking heart that the red light would draw him inexorably on.

She brought out an iced Star beer with two glasses and put them on the table. Then she took him in her arms, and he surrendered easily, to her waxed alabaster skin and her cocoa-buttered breasts, and the bitter lime smell between her legs.

◊　◊　◊

From then on the routine hardly varied: school and swim, the driving lesson, and then back to her place. The Italian mass was all but forgotten.

"Shall I kneel for you?" she would whisper, and he would bury his face in her wiry reddish hair and submit to the will of deepest darkest Africa.

"You're coming back awfully late these days," his mother would say sharply.

"Late duty at school," he would mumble. But he was careful: dutifully he would wait in the next evening, chopping grapefruit for her marmalade so that she was pacified.

And so he oscillated happily, between Asian childishness at home and African adulthood, till the day Jack arrived, bringing with him the third phase of his current life, European adolescence.

"A terrible thing has happened to me," Jack told him when he went that day to the mock-Tudor mansion in his green Opel.

"I've fallen in love. With Bronwen." Bronwen's father was the Barclay's Bank manager and they lived at the back of Romesh's house, so the two back gardens ran into each other. "It hurts so much I can't sleep at night."

Romesh wanted to tell him his news in return, but he knew it wouldn't do: they were liberated back then in the Seventies, those white African kids, but they were not broad-minded: Jack would have been shocked. Nigerians to them meant the stewards in their houses, the barman at the Crocodile Club, the girls by the Hamdala looking for custom. They did not have names or faces, and they were certainly not for sleeping with. One night Jack and he had encountered a girl on the racecourse while walking from the Crocodile to the Polo Club.

"Man, you don' go for jig-jig?" she asked. Jack fingered the five naira note in his breast pocket and replied in perfect pidgin:

"Eh-heh Madame, I like for to jig-jig plenty much, but I don' go be having money. Dat de problem." The girl had heard the rustle of money and she came after them indignantly and they ran. Romesh had always thought it a cruel thing to do but he never said so: in the adolescent European world he inhabited currently it was a great joke and Jack was the hero of the hour.

Bronwen and he had flown back together on British Caledonian.

"We tried to make out under the blanket, but you know those old bags who pass for stewardesses - why is it that on British Caledonian they are always over forty? - they watched us like hawks. Right through the night. I think they organised relays."

They both giggled as they passed the fat joint back and forth, lazing away the afternoon in Jack's room. Hash was widely available, sold openly in the Kaduna market in wide calabashes. Their friend Sean had smuggled a whole talking drum full of the stuff back through Heathrow.

Bronwen's parents were giving a party that night, and Jack and he arranged to meet there after ten, 'to give the *gerries* - geriatrics - a chance to loosen up and do their own thing.' The sky was flamingo pink when he left Jack's, and velvet black by the time he got home.

After a dutiful dinner of pittu and fish curry and an hour of mind-numbing cut-throat bridge with his parents, he walked across, past the twelve grapefruit trees and the empty - alas it was Wednesday! - servants quarters. Through a clearing in the trees he could see Chinese lanterns strung across the neighbouring garden.

Inside the house Sister Raphael was doing the Latin Hustle. She wore a long green evening dress with white shamrocks all over. Jack hadn't arrived but Bronwen took him over to the supper table, eyes shining.

"Has he told you our news?"

Romesh nodded. There were steaks and barbecued chicken wings and potato salad. He piled up a plate: in those days he could eat two or three dinners at a sitting and still manage to look lean and hungry.

"How's the maths going then?" Sister Raphael joined him at the table. She taught history at St. John's, aptly, Romesh thought, because she exuded an aura of a woman with a past.

"Bit of a struggle," he replied truthfully. he did not know to what Convent she belonged: she floated about the school all day. She was also to be found occasionally floating in the Hamdala pool, a cigarette in a long holder stuck in her mouth.

"How come I never see you in church?" he asked boldly, the first brandy-ginger beginning to take effect.

"Oh dear me no! I never go to them Eye-talian services. All that foreign mumbo-jumbo. Give me a good old-fashioned English mass any day. This trifle has too much rum in it," she said disapprovingly, changing the subject and giving herself a generous second helping.

"But that's *precisely* what I like about it: not being able to understand what's being said. The mysticism… No?"

She shot him a suspicious look and went back to her gerries.

"So when's the big day, then?" he asked Bronwen.

"Oh not yet, not just yet. Jack's got to become proficient with the animals, and I have to master my keyboard." Jack was training to be a vet and she a secretary, in Edinburgh. He looked at her enviously. Her life was like a hand of bridge that you laid down after a few tricks: I lose this and this and this, and then I win all the rest. It was easy, it was obvious: marriage to Jack, children, old age. Why was it so difficult for people like him, he thought unhappily. What did happiness mean anyway? The terraced house in Edinburgh with the children and the two dogs? The nine-to-five with the family back in Colombo? Maybe my happiness lies here, he thought even more unhappily, among the deep smoky colours of Africa, and the smell of bitter limes.

◊ ◊ ◊

When he got to the pool the next day with Jack, she scratched him softly on the palm of his hand as she gave him his free ticket.

"I have to see you," she whispered. He was annoyed. He almost asked 'Why?' meaning, 'can't you leave me be, in my adolescence?' But he stopped himself in time.

"Later," he whispered, "after this."

When he got to her the sun had already set. It was dark and he stumbled on the stairs. She was waiting for him at the top, a saint with a halo of sausage flies circling round the dim light bulb behind her head.

She had three thin chops on the grill - two for him, one for her - spiced with the fiery small chillies of West Africa. His two chops went down hardly touching the sides.

She was restless, on edge. His kisses strayed over her, down beyond her navel, licking up the cocoa-butter. She wriggled.

"What's wrong?"

"Nothing." She laughed. "Just the chilli on your tongue." But afterwards she was silent for a long while.

"I have something to tell you," she said. "I have missed."

He felt slightly sick. "What do you mean?" But he knew, even before she said it.

"It's ten days now. I'm normally very regular."

"Can't you get it fixed? I thought out here..." For no reason at all a picture of the dim chapel, the chanting priests, floated into his mind.

"You mean because it's primitive out here, it's easier to get a back street abortion?"

The coarseness of her words, her directness, stung him to the quick. He shrugged helplessly.

"Anyway I'm not sure I want an abortion."

He looked at her angrily. Was this the life that Africa had planned out for him, in this chocolate coloured room, behind the glass bead curtain?

"It's not such a big deal out here," she continued.

"Oh do what you want," he said angrily and stormed out.

◊   ◊   ◊

"Smoke up! Smoke up, Romesh me old darling!" said Jack. They were in the little bit of rough patch behind the Hamdala, next to the giant dustbins under the Indian almond trees. All around them there were vultures in shabby coats, pecking away at the rubbish and giving them all-knowing looks, like so many poor relations at a wedding.

"Got to keep our strength up. We have a long night ahead." The expat locusts were planning a tour of Kaduna's seedy nightspots.

"So much roast chicken, so little time," murmured Jack looking wistfully at the vultures. It was commonly rumoured that the chicken served in the Hamdala dining room, meaty and fibrous, was actually vulture.

Seedy nightspot meant anywhere other than the Kaduna or Crocodile or Polo clubs. They headed off in convoy, the green Opel leading.

"You can take this," said Jack, putting the little packet wrapped in cigarette foil into Romesh's shirt pocket. "You look the most innocent. They'll never search you."

They stopped at the Costain first. Instead of Elton John and Kiki Dee they were playing King Sunny Ade and Fela Ransome Kuti. They passed through a crowded bar. There was dancing in the open courtyard behind. A large sign in tinselled letters on the wall said 'Dancing with the members of the same sex not allowed.'

"Is *your* member of the same sex? Jack asked, slapping Romesh's behind.

They all joined hands and did the *highlife*. This is very easy to do: you half crouch on your knees, shuffle your feet and wiggle your bottom. The bigger the bottom the better the result: there were some spectacular highlifers there that evening.

Then onwards and downwards. They went up the main street, past Iossofidis - Romesh didn't even look up at her window - and into the native quarter. Some of the girls were getting nervous. They stopped at a barn-like structure lit by a pale blue neon light, vaguely reminiscent of the college chapel. In the gloom inside - gents one naira, ladies free - there were circular zinc tables. A series of open rooms led off the main hall, like side chapels in a church, where statuesque women sat motionless, like great baroque altarpieces. There were curtains drawn across some of the rooms, wherever service was in progress.

The locusts huddled in the middle, unable to talk over the boom-boom of the music. They were served Star beer at - daylight robbery - two naira apiece. As Romesh watched, a curtain across a side chapel was drawn aside and a familiar figure walked out. He sashayed past their table, a bemused gleam in his eyes.

"Good evening sir."

"Evening Ogun." Romesh thought sadly: two months ago I would have taken him aside and lectured him soundly on the morality of patronising a place like this, but I can't even do that now.

He had not visited Sindy for almost a week. She gave him his daily pool ticket without the slightest reproach in her eyes. He would take it and slink past, not looking back. She never charged him.

His eighteenth birthday was approaching, and his mother became even more wrapped up in her bridge and marmalade.

"You're old enough now, Romesh," she said. "Birthdays are only for *children*." All the same he felt sad. It fell on a Monday and his mother was busy with Sunday. Very busy. Jack had asked him over for a drink. When he got there in the green Opel something seemed to be going on. The mansion was floodlit and there were charcoal braziers all along the drive. Jack's mother stood at the door, gin and tonic in hand.

"Welcome," she said, "welcome." Then she lost the thread of her speech and wandered off uncertainly, a drunken guest in her own house.

He went through the hall and out onto the terrace, and down the three steps to the pool. As if by prior arrangement the music reared up at him:

'Say I'd like to know where,
You got the notion...'

"*Happy Birthday!*" screamed the locusts. That scene, the acid-green pool, the dancers framed by the firelight against the black African night, would stay etched in his memory for the rest of his life.

There was pepper chicken and jolloff rice, ofufu stew and those little deep-fried cakes called kuli-kulis: African food at its finest.

Jack and Bronwen put their arms round his shoulders and they danced in a circle at the edge of the pool. Bob Dylan was singing, 'Knock knock knocking on heaven's door.'

"We'll always stay like this, won't we?" they asked happily, but he did not answer. His mind was far away in the darkness of Africa, beyond the ruby red of the glass beads, buried deep in the lime of his bitter memories.

I have to see her, he said to himself all throughout classes the next day. The itch was so great that he left halfway through his English-as-a-foreign-language class that afternoon.

Mrs. Shaq popped out of the woodwork.

"You're leaving," she objected.
"I don't give a faq,
        Mrs. Shaq," he replied sweetly.

The priests were filing into church as he walked past, and he ignored them too.

Sindy was surprised to see him.

"I have something to tell you," he began. "What I mean is, if you really want..."

She held up her hand and smiled.

"You don't have to say anything more. It was a false alarm."

"You mean?"

"Yes, yes! I was just very late, that's all."

"But why didn't you tell me?"

She looked at him sharply. "Would it have mattered? You made your position very clear that day." He made as if to protest but she continued, "Anyway it wouldn't have made the slightest difference. I had already decided that I wanted to keep the baby. You know, Romesh, out here in Africa a mother and child are just that, and nothing more. There is nothing shocking or degrading about there being no father. You Westerners talk about liberation and empowerment for women, and we Africans laugh: it is we who are liberated and empowered, because we're not bound by your petty laws of so called morality and decency."

It was the longest speech she had ever made.

"I am not a Westerner," he said dully.

She laughed. "Anyway, you didn't think you were the only one, did you?"

"What's that?" he asked, shocked.

"You didn't think I waited for you, day in, day out, on the off-chance you might drop in after your bloody church service?" He looked as if he was about to burst into tears, and she relented. "But you *were* the only one I told. Because I thought you might, there might..." She fumbled for the words, her pride getting the better of her.

But he was not to be appeased. She watched him with her magnificent African eyes, clear and fathomless, as he left her, perhaps for the last time: he had just walked through the little glass bead into the red light beyond, leaving his youth and childhood far behind, into an adult world where there was betrayal at every step, a knife at every back.

When he drove past the savannah the beat of the Costain Club entered his head like a nagging toothache, but he ignored it: he had unfinished business to attend to.

The church was deserted. He pushed the door and it swung open silently. He went inside, and standing in the gloom at the back he began to pray,

"Ô Signore, non sono degno..."

The Night Bus To Clapham

Ashoka washed the champagne glasses with care. You had to be careful with them because they were fragile and rather too narrow to fit over the revolving brush of the glass-washer. Peter didn't like it if you broke anything. Not that he would deduct it from your pay, but he hated waste of any sort. It wasn't often that the champagne glasses were brought out of their corner from the rack overhead. Very few members could afford the club champagne: only the management, who had no qualms about ordering it because they did not have to pay. It was on the house. Ashoka could see them out of the corner of his eye at a table not far from the bar. He didn't dare look up because Peter would catch his eye and wink at him.

Peter was fat and spoke as if his mouth was full of *pittu*. He was one of the owners of the club. Ashoka put the glasses away carefully, standing on tip-toe to reach their place at the back of the rack. He shot a covert glance at the table. The management was out in full force: Peter, Alan, Sam and a woman with blonde hair. A member had once complained that the trouble with the club was that it had too many chiefs and not enough Indians. It occurred to Ashoka that the only Indian for miles around was himself. Alan must have been telling one of his dirty jokes at that moment because they all leant back and laughed. Even the blonde woman. Ashoka liked Alan because he always had a kind word for his employees.

"I like people from your part of the world," he said to Ashoka. "They're good workers. In fact, as far back as I can remember I've liked wogs."

Ashoka went round the corner to serve the other section. It was very quiet. A young man and his girlfriend were trying to do the crossword at the bar. The only lively quantity that night was the barrel of Carlsberg. An aged member, drinking white wine and soda, held out his glass for Ashoka to refill.

"Fifty-five pence please," said Ashoka courteously, and thought to himself, what am I doing here? When he went round the corner to ring the cash on the till he noticed the blonde woman sitting at the bar on her own. She was leaning her breasts on the bar and her shoulders were hunched. "When you're ready," she said to him. Her little-girl-lost air made Ashoka feel strong and silent, but instead he said out loud, "What will you have?"

Her mouth pursed in a lazy moment of indecision. "Port and lime juice, I think." Her voice had a slightly foreign slur, which made Ashoka feel funny in the small of his back. He poured the port carefully and measured out a shot of lime cordial.

"Don't you have lime juice?" she asked pouting. Not really blonde, Ashoka thought. More the colour of tarnished silver.

"I'm afraid not." He shook his head.

"Leave it then!" Her voice was peremptory, suddenly commanding. "I'll have a martini and lemonade." He was about to tell her she would have to pay for both but he remembered in time. She was with Peter and Alan, and however many ports she decided not to have, they would all be on the house, like the champagne.

"Where do you come from?" she asked.

"Sri Lanka."

"And your name?"

"Jonathan."

She smiled, saying, "How funny! I didn't expect you to have an English name." He would have liked to point out how it was not only funny, but false too, but it would have been no use. She would have asked for his real name and promptly forgotten it. Jonathan was simpler and more convenient. And though it was a lie each time he said it, it was well within the rules of the game: you were in a certain situation at a certain time in the presence of certain people; but you were *in* their company, not *of* it. For them it did not matter who you were, only that you were present and therefore required some explanation. Even then it was not the truth they were after but plausibility: and that is what you gave them; though you had to be strict with yourself and not be self-indulgent. They had a right to as much of you as they could take without choking. So you could dress up the truth to make it more palatable but you had to go easy on the garlic. And if, one day, they were able to accept all of you as you actually were, then, only then, could they be your friends.

It had been like that for as long as he could remember. Once the glasses were washed and put away and he was on the night bus back to Clapham, he could be Ashoka again. For the space of a bus ride.

"Thank you." She lowered her eyes gratefully to the martini and lemonade. It was time to go and collect the plates off the tables, but she had her glass on the flap that led out from the bar, and also an elbow. She smiled mischievously at his consternation. "Crawl through," she said pointing to the gate underneath the flap. He opened the gate and taking care not to spill her drink he crept through. Her hand rested for a moment between his shoulder-blades and again he felt funny in the small of his back. Taking care to avoid Peter's side of the table, Ashoka collected the plates.

"I like Orientals because they're good workers," Alan said. "See that you take good care of my wife."

Wife? Ashoka thought as he went into the kitchen with the plates. The tarnished blonde of course. He hadn't realized Alan was married. He stacked up the plates neatly and went back to the bar. This time he didn't wait for her to move. He pushed open the gate and began to crawl through but she stretched out a leg in his way and he got past with the greatest difficulty.

"How do you feel?" she asked impishly.

"Fine," he replied, angry and desirous in equal parts. Desirous, because desirability was one of her more prominent assets, and angry because she had broken the unwritten rule by demanding more than plausibility. Resisting the urge to ravish her on the spot he vanished round the corner to the other side of the bar.

But there was no peace there for him either.

"Countrymen who could be great barkers?" asked the girl at the crossword.

"Danes," muttered Ashoka disapprovingly and escaped before she could ask another. Damn clever, these wogs. The blonde ordered another martini and downed it quickly. Her voice became more slurred, more foreign.

"Do you live alone?" she asked.

He shook his head. "With my family." Was that within the rules? Probably not, he thought, I must concentrate, be disciplined, or I shall lose myself entirely. He felt sad, like someone who has caught himself cheating at patience.

"Isn't that awfully dull?" she asked.

"Awfully," he replied with a smile, but it wasn't her idea of a joke.

"What's the matter, don't you like me?" She was quite tipsy by now. She reached out with both hands, pulled his face towards her and kissed him. He looked with concern towards Alan, but Alan had his back turned and she dismissed him with a wave of her hand. "Forget him. He and I, we have this…" she hesitated over the choice of words, "…this *arrangement*. But don't you like me?" To say no would not have been permissible so he turned round to wash some more glasses.

"What's your excuse anyway?" she called out. "Do you prefer Peter?"

"My excuse," he smiled furiously, "is total and absolute innocence."

"It's not possible," she said in disbelief; but she meant 'plausible,' and anyway it was true.

He always felt outside the place and time in which he existed, so he could never be responsible for his actions, good or bad. A wise man cannot be held to blame in the company of fools, nor a fool in the company of wise men.

"Just think of all the things I could teach you," she began, but he would not listen and she grew exasperated. "I can't understand how you can be so pretty and still refuse me." An agonised cry out of the depths, from the boss's wife who has never been refused anything.

It was nearly midnight, Cinderella time. If he didn't hurry he would miss the night bus to Clapham. He was washing up the plates in the kitchen when Peter shimmered up to him, like a goblin on Halloween night. "Tonight's the night!" he said lusciously. Ashoka pushed him aside and went back to the bar.

"You think I'm too old for you, don't you?" Her little girl's voice was plaintive, whining. He did not answer, not because it was an unusual complaint. On the contrary he had heard it many times before.

Yet, as he shivered at the bus-stop he half hoped she would appear in her chauffeur-driven car and whisk him away to some warm room, any room, anywhere, he thought, but Clapham. But she was probably still at the bar nursing her disappointment with martinis or listening to her husband's dirty stories.

When he got back home, Olivia was waiting up for him with a hot meal.

"Darling Jonathan," she said, for he was Ashoka only for the space of a bus-ride. She kissed him on the lips and sat him down. Her hair was gold too, but streaked in a dignified sort of way, not tarnished.

"How was work?" she asked brightly.

"Bloody awful," he replied non-committally. At this she grew vexed.

"How many times do I have to tell you? At forty-three, I am old enough and rich enough to look after both of us "

Jiggy

"**A** nd there is no doubt that you'll be tempted!*" thundered the lay preacher, looking round aggressively and daring anyone in the audience to defy him. The man next to me was getting agitated.

"But you must remember, the essence of marriage is to travel the rocky path, looking neither left nor right at the luscious fruit you'll be passing on either side." He dwelt lovingly on the word 'luscious.' No doubt he had been tempted many a time himself. My soon-to-be wife squeezed my hand reassuringly. We had been sent by our parish priest to attend this marriage guidance course a week before the wedding, and so far only the bad bits had been mentioned.

Our neighbour meanwhile had turned to look at us. Or more specifically, at me. He could barely keep the excitement out of his voice.

"I've seen you before!" His voice got louder. "Last month. At St. Mary's, Dehiwala. You were having your *son* baptized!" The whole class looked on in scandalized wonder. The preacher was dumbstruck.

"So you've been down this particular road before, have you?" asked my future wife sharply as the lecture ended in chaos...

This was my first introduction to Jiggy. After much protest I had got my neighbour to admit that the man he had seen at St. Mary's was bigger than me, and fairer, and therefore *not* me. "But he looks exactly like you," he insisted.

They say that everybody has a double somewhere in the world and they are lucky if they come across him once in their lifetime. Well I am blessed, or cursed, with a double who lives in the same town as me, a one-horse town called Colombo. His name is Jiggy. What fun, you think. Well, believe me, it's not.

Jiggy lived an entirely different life to me. Bright red cars, fast clubs and Colombo 7 women, or do I mean fast cars, Colombo 7 clubs and bright red women? I, on the other hand, live in Pannipitiya with a wife, a kid and two cats. I am an accountant. How much more different can you get? Yet at least once a week for the last ten years I have been stopped on the street by perfect strangers claiming to have seen me, in usually quite unacceptable circumstances. And if you detect a whiff of disapproval in that last sentence you're damn right. Us accountants have our reputation to keep up.

Jiggy was obviously a two-bit chancer living off his wits, a bit of acting work here, a bit of modelling work there, but nothing respectable or decent or regular. I didn't meet him for years, but like those computer artists who draw faces by putting thousands of little x's on lines, I had built up a pretty good picture long before I did. Now don't get me wrong. You can hardly object, can you, if you're mistaken for an actor or whatever on the streets? But to me my job is sacred, and the day the whole office stood up hooting and jeering when I walked in, that's the day it really got to me.

"I say machang, give us a peep!"

"Never thought you had it in you, old boy!"

"What are you talking about?" I asked.

"Don't pretend to be so innocent!" they shrieked. "That exhibition of male nudes at Gallery 706 by that woman photographer? There is a smashing one of you there with your lunch-packet hanging out!"

Useless to tell them it wasn't me. I escaped with difficulty to my room. Room when you say, three plywood partitions reaching up to about shoulder height that separated me from the common herd. But they all remained outside, clapping and wolf whistling.

"Never apologize, never explain," said Marianne my secretary when she came in with my files.

"Not you too! Surely you don't think that I..."

"If you've got it, flaunt it," she said sweetly as she left the room.

Worse was to come when I got home. My wife was on the phone to the Hog. Before I go any further, let me explain that my wife is an old girl of Ladies College, and very proud she is of it too. In fact she is a member of the Old Girls Association. Their President, the Head Old Girl or Hog as we call her, is always on the phone about some committee matter or other.

My wife signalled frantically. "Don't go," she whispered, "she wants to have a word with you." My heart sank.

"That's quite right, Daphne," my wife was saying into the phone, "now if you just hold on for a moment, I'll hand you over to him - yes he's just here."

Cautiously I took the phone.

"Hullo Asoka?" the Hog was brisk and businesslike. "Only one thing I wanted to say, the next time you feel the irresistible urge to expose yourself to the camera do remember you're married to an old girl of Ladies College, all right?"

"But it wasn't me!"

"No of course not, it was your double, your spitting image. That's what they all say when they get caught," and she rang off.

It was then that I decided things had gone far enough. But events were about to overtake me. The next day was my weekly Rotary lunch at the Hilton, an event I look forward to because it gives me the chance to wear my one good gray suit.

"That was a quick change," commented the doorman as I walked in.

"What do you mean?"

"Well you just walked past here in jeans a minute ago."

"And where was I going?"

The doorman gave me an odd look.

"You went towards the Pub there, sir," he said pointing. I hesitated for a moment. I felt like a man who is about to meet his mail-order bride after many months of correspondence.

"Courage, O Rotarian," I said to myself, and girding my loins I walked in through the swing doors of the Hilton Pub. I spotted him immediately. The funny thing is, he really did look like me. He was even wearing the sort of clothes I would have worn at the weekend.

"Ah the accountant from Funny Pitiya!" he said looking at me speculatively.

"How do you know I'm from funny - I mean Pannipitiya?" I asked angrily.

"I followed you there once. That's how." This was really too much. "You were on the 138 bus, and there was a big crush. I know I shouldn't have, but I couldn't resist. Just to see how the other half lives." He grinned. "By the way, your wife is cute."

"You leave my wife out of this!"

"Anyway don't worry, I didn't have to pay. The conductor thought I was you."

"So what did you think?" I asked, curious in spite of myself. He threw up his hands in horror.

"Funny Pitiya," he said. Just that.

"Well you can talk!" I countered. "You ought to be ashamed of yourself, the life you lead! You're getting me into all sorts of trouble."

"Me getting *you* into trouble?" He asked incredulously. "What about *me*? How do you think I feel when people say they've seen me on the 138 bus?" He shuddered involuntarily. "I have a reputation to keep up, you know. I've been seen buying children's party hats at Arpico, and listen, the other day a girl even saw me at the vet's with two cats. Cats, I ask you!"

"We are getting off the point," I said hastily. You know who I am, so you'd better tell me who you are."

"People call me Jiggy," he said shaking my hand, "and I live on Flower Road."

"Oh, very posh," I murmured.

"Yes, isn't it. I have a room in my landlady's house." He smirked. "She advertised half a bed to let, or was it a room with a view, I can't remember."

"I didn't know Flower Road had views," I said.

"Don't you believe it! I'm directly opposite Ladies College. A man couldn't ask for a better view than that."

"All I wanted to tell you," I said, getting up, "was that next time you want to do nude pictures please think of my reputation."

"Where are you going?" He asked with an injured air, "I was just beginning to enjoy our little chat..."

I left him. I had to pop into the gents on the way to the Rotary lunch, but when I looked up, I saw the cheeky sod had followed me in. There must have been ten urinals in the place but he had to choose the one next to mine.

"Anyway," I said as I finished doing my business, "I'm glad to see that in one respect at least we're not at all alike. You're only half the man I am!"

"We can't all be as lucky as you," he said eyeing me reproachfully.

"Besides it's not what you've got, it's what you do with it. That's what all the girls tell me."

"Is *that* what they tell you? Ha!" And so saying, I made my victorious exit.

Back at home, things returned to normal. The mother-in-law came to stay.

"Never trust a man who doesn't like cats," she said examining their bellies for boot marks. She does this every time she comes. All because once, when they wouldn't get off my favourite chair, I gave them a surreptitious kick and got caught out. My mother-in-law comes from a long line of cat-lovers, or should that read, cats? In her house I am known as the Cat-kicker. It isn't nice.

At Keells the boy at the meat counter wanted me to teach him karate.

"Karate?" I asked him blankly.

"Why, Master, you were demonstrating katas on TV the other night?"

"Oh that," I said airily. "That's nothing." Jiggy's fame was beginning to rest lightly on my brow. But there was no doubt his jobs were getting more bizarre by the day.

At the weekend we went shopping at Elephant House. (Oh the dizzy social whirl of the middle-aged married man.) Halfway between the toothpastes and the thosai mixes I was assaulted - no other word for it - by a woman in a thambili-orange trouser suit.

"Darling," she said. "*Darling*. Thursday night was super. *Do* let's do it again, soonest."

While this full and frank exchange of views was taking place, who should come round the corner but the wife, with a frozen chicken in her hand. I tell you she may be cute, my wife, but she sure throws a mean chicken. I was in the doghouse or do I mean cat-litter for at least a week.

But even that episode was forgiven or forgotten after a while. The Hog did call once, begging my wife please to ask me not to loiter at the Ladies College gates with my tongue hanging out, as I had been seen by Many Old Girls (Mogs). But even the wife was getting hardened to these accusations and beginning to take them less seriously.

I didn't actually see Jiggy again for quite a few months. Then Marianne my secretary decided to have a birthday bash at the Rock Café. I dropped in after work on the way home and there he was, a solitary figure in the garden. I took my drink and joined him.

"Hi there!" he said glumly, "What brings you here?"

"Jiggy, just because I live in Pannipitiya doesn't mean to say I don't have a social life you know."

"Doesn't it?"

I let that one pass. "I am here for my secretary Marianne's birthday. Are you a friend of hers too?"

"No, but maybe you can give me an introduction," he said hopefully.

"Jiggy, don't you have a wife and child at home - the one you had christened at St. Mary's?"

He looked blank for a moment.

"Oh that! That's ancient history. I gave her the boot, or rather," he said telling the truth for once in his life, "she gave me the boot. She's in Dubai now, with the kid."

"What's she doing there?"

"Duty free shopping, for all I care."

"Jiggy what do you really want from life? What are you actually looking for?" The drink must have been working inside me. I'm not normally this serious, not even in Pannipitiya.

Jiggy was silent for a long while. "You know what I really want?" He looked at me. "I want to be you."

"What! with a wife and kid and two cats?" I could hardly believe my ears.

"That too. But I want to be serious like you and wear a gray suit and go to Rotary lunches. I want to be a man of substance. The trouble is, I want the glamour too, the women, the cars and all that."

"Jiggy, listen to me, you can't have both. You know that. Look at all these social butterflies," I said, thinking particularly of the woman in the thambili trouser suit, "they've spread themselves out so thin, there's nothing left to them any more, just a bright shiny shell. You crack it and there's nothing inside, just empty space."

"You're a fat lot of help, you are!"

"If you can't go back to your first wife find yourself another," I said, warming to my theme. "Wives are strange animals. If you're good to them, they're good back. If you're bad to them, they're evil."

"Thank you for those pearls of wisdom," he grinned. "I'll try to keep them in mind."

I took the 138 bus back home, and it was packed. As I extricated my nose from someone else's armpit, I thought with just a tinge of regret, about Jiggy's fast cars and bright red women. Just a tinge, mind you, just a tinge.

Christmas came, and we spent it with the wife's family. Nothing of note happened, except that I got drunk and insulted the mother-in-law's cat. And then I had to go and spoil it all by winning the office lottery. This usually takes place once a year, and the money collected is spent on some needy cause, like feeding the poor of Cinnamon Gardens, or rehabilitating fallen nuns, or running hairdressing courses for bald men. Anyway the prize was brilliant, a weekend for two at Kandalama Hotel. If you haven't been to Kandalama, let me tell you it is spectacular, a hotel cut into the rock face, a modern day Sigiriya fortress. We boarded the kid with the mother-in-law who also promised to feed the cats, and headed off *à deux* into the sunrise, armed with cutlets and boiled eggs.

The receptionist gave me a wide smile when I arrived. "Wasn't that your brother who just checked in?" she asked. "Such a charming guy!"

"Oh?" was all I could manage in my state of shock. Luckily the wife was out of earshot. She was toiling up the steps with our four and a half pieces of luggage, which she had refused to entrust to the porter. She likes to travel light.

Trust the beggar to ruin our weekend, I thought, as we were shown to our room. Kandalama has views to die for, with acres of jungle and lake spread out before you, and monkeys swinging from tree to tree. I went out on the balcony, put down the box of cutlets, took off my shades and made myself comfortable on the sun lounger. The wife went off for her bath. From where I was I could just see a corner of the pool. Girls in bikinis were shrieking as they leapt in and out. Somewhere in their midst, no doubt, was Jiggy...

I must have dozed off, because a moment later I was woken up by an almighty scream. I rushed into the bathroom where the wife lay frozen in the bathwater. There was a monkey outside the window in my sunglasses. As we watched, he finished the last of the cutlets and threw the box away. Then he took my sunglasses off, hurled them into the jungle and vanished.

I was outraged. "Never mind!" said the wife, "the monkey looked better in those glasses than you ever did."

Dinner that night was a magnificent affair: the mellow candle-lit dining room with its stark black iron trees rising from the timber floor, all set against a dramatic backdrop of floodlit rock; a far cry from Pannipitiya. If only Jiggy could see me now, I thought, as we sat down to our lobster at a discreet table behind a column. I patted the brand new credit card in my shirt pocket to reassure myself: the free weekend included the buffet dinner, but any extras, like the lobster, I would have to pay for myself.

Suddenly the iron tree behind us started to sing.

"Funnee... Pitiya..." it sang, "Funnee... Pitiya..."

"It must be this dry zone air," said the wife. "There's this funny sort of singing in my ears." I was just about to go round the corner and thump him, when the singing stopped.

"Oh that's better," said the wife shaking her ears. "For a minute there I thought I was losing it."

The next morning the wife put on her frilly two-piece and settled herself by the pool with her favourite book, "One hundred ways with frozen chicken." I headed off to the gym.

"What's happened to you?" asked the trainer eyeing my baggy shorts critically. "You were in such smart gym clothes yesterday. And that stomach! It was flat as a board!"

"It must be all your good hotel food," I said. "Now buzz off."

Soon enough, the weekend came to an end. Jiggy had thankfully avoided us throughout. When I went to settle the bill, the nice receptionist held out two envelopes.

"This one is for your extras, and this," she said, "is your brother's bill."

My blood ran cold.

"Where is he?"

"He just checked out with that party of girls." She pointed out a jeep in the middle distance, disappearing in a cloud of dust.

"All he said was, *'Aiya will pay.'*" Sweetly she handed me the bill. The hotel was our firm's best client, and I was the firm's junior partner. How could I make a fuss? I pulled out the credit card with trembling fingers. I never told the wife.

Even today, years later, I still wonder why I paid. I could have refused. I could have insisted it was nothing to do with me. It would have been easy enough, after all, to track him down to his lair in Flower Road. But if there is one thing us accountants are not trained to cope with it is embarrassment. And ultimately, I know that all the fuss would have reflected badly on me. So I paid up and shut up.

But I was furious all the same. This town was really not big enough for both of us. I returned to Colombo an unhappy man. The weekend in Kandalama, however, had done the wife a world of good. She even began to smile at me. Now and then. In office a week later, Marianne popped her head round the door.

"Jiggy called," she said. "He wants to meet you urgently this evening at six, at the Rock."

"Jiggy? How does he have this number?"

"I gave it to him. The night of my birthday." A dreamy look came into her eyes. "I gave him my home number as well." The man was a menace. He was slowly taking over my life. I went to meet him that evening, determined to have it out with him.

"Ah, just the man I wanted to see," he said. "I've been thrown out of my lodgings."

"What happened?" I asked with a certain sense of satisfaction,

"Couldn't pay your rent?"

He smiled. "I never did pay any rent. The truth is, the landlady had certain high hopes of me." He paused, embarrassed. "But I never could come up to her expectations."

It was my turn to smile. "So where are you now?"

"I'm at a friend's place. She said I could crash out for the weekend. That was two weeks ago and I'm still there. Any day now she'll throw me out too."

"And then?"

There was a pause. "Perhaps you could put me up?" he suggested helpfully. "I've always wanted to live with an accountant and two cats."

"Are you out of your mind?" I got angry. "Look Jiggy, you can't go on with this hand-to-mouth existence. Get yourself a decent job. Get real. How about applying for something in the Middle East?"

"Funny you should say that. I've been offered a job as a life-guard at a hotel in Saudi. Do you think I should take it?"

"Take it. Please, please, take it!"

"There's only one problem. The job agency wants 25,000." Then an idea struck him. "You wouldn't be able to lend me ten would you? You see I can lay my hands on the balance fifteen. I'd pay you back, promise."

"Sure. Like your hotel bill at Kandalama."

He looked up and laughed. "Yes, well, sorry about that. It was all Marianne's idea. Blame her."

"Marianne? What's she got to do with it?"

"If you must know, she's the friend I've been staying with."

"The sneaky so-and-so! She never said anything..."

"Well she wouldn't, would she? She wouldn't want to get into trouble with the boss."

It was all getting to be too much for me. I dug deep into my pocket. The funny thing is that I actually did have five thousand in there. I had taken it out that morning for the cats' hysterectomies. The vet likes to be paid in cash.

"Look, Jiggy, I'm willing to help you out. But not ten. Here's five, and you'll somehow have to find yourself the balance." The cats would have to wait. "And you'll have to promise me you'll take the job and not spend the money on anything else."

"How come you're walking around with so much money in your pocket?" he asked curiously. Unwillingly, I told him. Promising on all the gods that he would take the job and not get sidetracked, he got up to go.

"Take care, my friend," I said, hugging him. "Earn yourself lots of money. And remember, this is the surest way back to Pannipitiya and all that." He gave me an odd, unhappy look.

"And may your cats have ever more kittens," he said vanishing into the gloom.

I never did hear from him again. As the months went by people stopped recognizing me on the streets, and the service I got in shops sank to its usual, less than gracious levels. Life became boringly, mind-numbingly normal. Deadliest of all, the Hog was actually beginning to get quite fond of me. She told me I was a changed man and that she considered me one of her finest success stories. ("One word from me and you were as right as rain.") I got promoted at work, from a plywood partition to an asbestos one. The woman in thambili, alas, was nowhere to be seen.

I realized with a pang that I was actually missing him. Was I right in sending him away? Although I hardly knew him, I also knew that I was the one person he had listened to. Do any of us have the right to play God in other people's lives? Marianne, for one, certainly blamed me.

"It's the best thing that could happen to him," I once said to her. "You'll see, it'll really make a man of him." She turned her eyes on me and they were like flame-throwers. I retreated hastily behind the asbestos.

A year must have passed. Then one day the girl at the Keells fish counter gave me a pouty look.

"I gave you my number at least a week ago. You still haven't rung."

"My number?" I asked with a sudden unaccountable lightening of the heart. "Did you say you gave me your number? Well just be patient," I smiled. "If I said I'll be in touch, I'll be in touch."

Oudenarde and Malplaquet, Ramillies and Blenheim

"And the next time you put too much sugar in my coffee you're out of here, you understand? Out, out, *out!*" Every day she does this to me because she's trying to kill me, I know that. She and I are the last ones left, and it's a sort of competition to see who can last longest. But however much I shout at her she never goes. She has nowhere else to go, probably.

My grandmother brought Ros back from the convent when she was very young. She simply told the Mother

Superior, I'm going to adopt six of your orphans, and just brought them back. Adoption was as simple as that in those days. The Convent was part of our petty fiefdom anyway, being built at the bottom of the garden, by the sea. She gave them names: Ros and Josie, Poppy and Sita, Mary and Marie, like so many creatures out of a nursery rhyme.

Ros is the last one left.

Then there is me. I am Catherine de Silva, named after my great ancestor Catherine, my grandmother's cousin. She was the heiress who married Sir Charles Henry de Soysa. They say he was after my grandmother first, but she was tall and fair, and he was small and sickly, so he did not stand a chance. Catherine was the consolation prize. And *what* a consolation! In those days they were like royalty around here. When Queen Victoria's son the Duke of Edinburgh dropped in for dinner they fed him off solid gold plate, they say, and the gold knives and forks were inlaid with rubies and pearls.

Catherine and my grandmother were both born in this house. It is called *Malplaquet* and it belongs to me now. The house of course predates them all by a hundred years at least.

Malplaquet and Oudenarde, Ramillies and Blenheim, the names would roll trippingly off my grandmother's tongue those days when I was a child. They were the names *her* grandfather had repeated to her when *she* was a young girl, the names of the battles the great Churchill won for the Dutch and English against the Sun King. Ceylon belonged to the Dutch then, you see, and the house would have been built soon after, a sort of victory celebration in the backwoods of the Empire.

Every morning I sit in the kitchen verandah of Malplaquet, in the milky morning air of the seaside, on an old wooden thunderbox, which I hasten to add hasn't been used the way it was originally intended, for at least half a century! There are no devils to bother me at this hour. Ros sits on a low stool and we drink our coffee in companionable enmity. There would have been a time in the old days when Ros was not allowed to sit in my presence, the laws of etiquette here at Malplaquet being as rigid as *Versailles,* but those days are long gone now. She does not call me '*hamu*,' or 'my lady' any more, though she does not call me Catherine. Yet.

I would not want you to get the wrong impression, though, by talking about Malplaquet in the same breath as *Versailles* or *Blenheim*. On the contrary, it is a pitiably small house with wooden columns and creaking baroque windows, and a smoke-blackened kitchen wing overlooking the coffee-trees and lovi-lovi bushes outside, that I tend to myself. I tell you, you haven't lived till you've tasted my wine-dark lovi jam, and my coffee is to die for, if Ros's doesn't kill you first. My secret is that I roast the beans in sand, but those secrets will die with me when I die. The house is built of wattle and daub, and all the doors are built in two halves, to keep the farm animals out. No farm animals now, unless you count Ros and me.

But I'm not ashamed of this house, you see, because this is how we all began life, we of the Fisher Dynasties, in the time of *Ramillies and Oudenarde, Malplaquet and Blenheim*. (Oh how those names reverberate in my head, like the beats of a drum!) There were barely a handful of us then, the de Soysas and de Mels, the Fernandos and de Silvas, and a few others. And this little seaside village called Moratuwa is where we all came from. It tickles me now to hear of Moratuwa talked about as a dreary suburb of Colombo, the capital, because as far as *we* are concerned, Colombo is a dreary suburb of Moratuwa.

And when I step out in my drop-waisted dresses and my clunky shoes amidst the sniggers of the new people, it gives me great satisfaction to walk through the better parts of Cinnamon Gardens and Havelock Town and know that every house, and I mean *every* house, belongs to a third, fourth or fifth cousin. And if they laugh at my outfits now, I think, they should have seen me *then* in my heyday, in my hat and gloves and most glorious of all, my stockings. I'll never forget the day, Easter Sunday, at St. Philip Neri's, when the Japanese bombed Colombo and we dived under the pews and I lost the bunch of grapes on my hat!

Mind you, we are a different race, we of the Fisher Dynasties, and not a pretty one at that. We are not the famous copper-coloured Sinhalese of the scriptures. Our colour is at least two octaves below that and our sharp eyes and flyaway hair give us all a mad look, none more mad than me I have to admit! Even today when I walk down the streets I can spot a relation, because they all have that particular air of home-made clumsiness that I have come to know and love.

But you cannot beat us for our deep understanding of money. It seems to grow on trees for our green-fingered race. When I was small they would bring it in gunny sacks and throw it in the end room there, sack after sack after sack, and at the end of the day there was so much money we had to push the sacks in really hard to get the door closed. This was the money from our arrack-rents, because, being Christian, we had no qualms about selling alcohol. It is interesting that rather late in the day some of my cousins have developed a conscience and embraced temperance, conveniently forgetting the very basis their fortunes were founded on.

But the thirty thousand acres of Lady de Soysa's time dwindled to four thousand in my father's day, and, what with land reform and poverty nipping delicately at my heels, I am now down to thirty seven. And you might as well be poor in style, I said to myself, and sold the lot. I had a great desire, you see, to visit the Imperial Capital before I died. So I cashed in the remaining acres and flew to London. I had an idea it would suit me better than Moratuwa. My great-nephew whom I stayed with found it all a bit of a hoot.

"Just wait till the winter comes," he said, "and you have to put the dustbins out on a freezing Thursday night. That'll make you change your mind and long for Moratuwa again."

But I did and I didn't. In fact I called our High Commissioner in London to the house - he was a nephew too so he could hardly refuse - and explained that I wanted to spend my last days there. I explained that London was more congenial to my temperament, and that the devils were giving me grief back at Malplaquet. At this he looked troubled and went away and I never heard from him again. But before my visa ran out I went to Harrods and bought myself a magenta silk dress with black polka dots on it, the high point of the trip, and, the other day, in a magazine I saw Princess Diana in virtually the identical dress.

I am back at Malplaquet now and the devils are getting worse. I can feel that it is time to take our last bow and leave the stage. The Fisher Dynasties have had their quarter millennium of fame when they held this country in the palm of their hand. In any case, I feel the rot set in when our descendants moved to Colombo and built themselves palaces, and generally got above themselves. Their blood is thinned now with too much copper and it is poisoning the system. Worst of all, they are losing their once sure touch with money.

I wonder what will become of Malplaquet when I die and my great-nephew takes over. Will he sell it for scrap and retire to London with the proceeds? Then again maybe not. It has stood for one quarter of a millennium, so why not another? Besides it is too small to attract the greedy eye of developers, cut up and hemmed in as it is, by Church and Convent, road and rail.

There is only one sure thing: when I die, only Ros will be there by my bedside. She may not be good for much but she has stood by me through thick and thin. The relations will only come later, when they are sure they won't be called upon to spend their good money on me. They will come to pick over the bones of my carcass...

The other day a young nun challenged me as I was taking a short-cut through the convent down to the beach.

"And who might *you* be?" she asked. She had a pretty, coppery, Kandyan face. I drew myself up to my full five-foot-nothing height.

"I am Catherine de Silva," I said, "and it is you who are on my land, not I on yours." I am glad to say she blushed to the roots of her wimple and fled. *O, but the times they are a-changing…*

Back at home it is dusk and the devils creep out of the shadows to plague me. In the courtyard of the Buddhist temple nearby they are drumming, because it is Poya day today. Ros has put on a spotless white sari, and really, she looks rather stunning, though I would die rather than tell her so. She has filled a siri-siri bag full of temple flowers and there is a faint flush to her cheeks. It is the drumming I know that gets her excited.

But to me it means nothing. For you see, my dear, in my mind I march to the beat of a different drum: it goes *Oudenarde and Malplaquet, Ramillies and Blenheim.*

Feng - Shui

I n the summer of 1983 Professor Jayaweera decided
to holiday in Miami.

"Colombo is *such* a bore!" Myra had said. "Every year
you go there and every year you come back complaining
about the heat and the flies and the mosquitoes. Try *our*
mosquitoes for a change." Myra was his best student. She
had graduated with an Upper Second and gone back to
Miami.

"Miami is hot, hot, hot!" she wrote. "Don't bring anything, just yourself." To prove her point she sent him pictures: Myra in running shorts running on the beach; Myra in cycling shorts cycling through the wooded lanes of Coconut Grove; and Myra in hot pants drinking a *café Cubano* beside a board which read *Se habla Inglés*. Lastly there was a shot of Myra, her red hair whipped up into a froth, sitting in the Jacuzzi in her back-yard in Mary Street. Professor Jayaweera looked closely to see whether she was wearing anything. He could not tell.

For most of his life Professor Jayaweera had lived in England, arriving as an impoverished student and staying on. He liked the sense of freedom and independence this gave, this conscious act of snipping off the umbilical cord. Outside of work he had no friends, no family, and he felt supremely free: there was no one to tell him how to behave or what to eat or what to wear. Back home everyone had opinions. Even the woman who sold fish door to door would not hesitate to tell you if she disliked the colour of your shirt or the cut of your hair. Here of course there was Myra who did her best, though alas, with very little success. Most of all, Professor Jayaweera loved those Western ideals of justice and fair play which allowed for this freedom of choice: not for him those sinuous *feng-shui* curves of Asian truth and half-truth which only served to bind you inextricably. Western justice ran in unbending lines, straight and true, like arrows to the horizon. And within the cage of those straight lines, it seemed to him, you were free as a bird and life was really rather simple indeed.

The flight to Miami was full. The passengers in the queue inched closer to the check-in. The woman behind kept nudging him forward, as if that would get him any sooner to the top. He turned round to protest, then changed his mind. Professor Jayaweera prided himself on his good manners and gentle behaviour, the civilising influences of England. The England of today was of course not the England he had come to in the Sixties, but Professor Jayaweera was determined to carry on as if it were. He prided himself that he had always been correct, had never crossed the line, as so many of his countrymen had done over the intervening years. How they looked up to him when he went back 'home' every year! How they envied him his English bearing and his English behaviour!

"Come back," they urged. "Now that you're Head of English over there, you can walk into any job over here. They'll kill to have you. You might even make V.C.!"

But the Professor did not rise to these suggestions. He knew that back in Sri Lanka he would have immense power and prestige as a returnee academic. But those little indulgences of everyday life, those little privileges and freedoms that he took for granted in the West would go. He knew only too well how those Eastern satraps loved to give with one hand and take away with the other: and they took away those freedoms by invoking the bigger pictures of Poverty or Terrorism or Universal Health; by appealing to your better nature and your social conscience. But the really funny part was that the man who took away those freedoms never dreamed of similarly depriving himself: the man who ordered the roadblocks would be outraged if he too had to stop at them. Then there was the man who levied those killer taxes who certainly never paid taxes himself, proud government servant that he was, supported by an ever-grateful paying public. And as for the man who was really rather sorry there were not nearly enough beds to go round in most state hospitals: well, *he* was really rather glad he could afford to take himself off to Singapore when *he* fell ill.

Thanks, thought the professor, but no thanks. I am a selfish little beast, and I'm really very happy where I am, in my two bedroomed house in North London, living alone.

"I would much rather," he told Myra, "be a small fish in a big pond than a big fish in a small one."

"I would much rather not be a fish at all," snapped Myra irritably.

The woman behind was trying to attract his attention. "Excuse me, sir," she said. TheProfessor noted with slight distaste the rolling American *r*, the handsome Hispanic face all hung about with gold jewellery, the bright blue turban. There was a gap between her front teeth.

"I couldn't help noticing that you have only one small suitcase. Could I ask you to check one of mine through?"

The professor looked doubtfully at her trolley. There were three enormous cases on it. He hesitated.

"Please," she begged, "it'll cost me so much in excess baggage otherwise."

"All right," he said. Professor Jayaweera knew then that he had done the right thing being helpful, and he was glad.

When he first came to London nobody had been particularly helpful to him and life had not been easy. He remembered the stringent economies of his Wandsworth bedsit, the curried cubes of Spam for lunch, the *parippu* soup taken with thin slices of toast for dinner. It had not been easy being a black man teaching English to the English. He remembered young Mr. Hart, his colleague at the Polytechnic, who asked him rather nastily, "I suppose you lot sit about cross-legged in your huts all day long, speaking English to each other?" But the professor had risen above all that.

To supplement his income he taught Sinhala to the sons of rich Sri Lankans who were boarded at British public schools. They came to him once a week, condescending and superior, not caring much whether they learned anything or not. Even to them he was kind, treating them to chocolate digestives and Jaffa cakes, things he never bought for himself. He felt he was in some small way giving something back to the motherland, keeping Sinhala alive in the minds of these fine young savages. And if they noticed the mildewed flock wallpaper in his room, or the torn carpet with the yellowing newspapers underneath they did not say. But the professor had come to grow quite fond of his little home. One rainy afternoon he had read all about the abdication of Edward VIII through a gap in the carpet.

All that was over now: he was Head of English, there was too much of a demand on his time. He had his own house. But, inexplicably, now that he could afford to eat virtually anything he wanted, he still hankered after those cubes of Spam, that thin *parippu* soup.

The woman heaved a particularly hideous suitcase, covered in a wildly improbable tartan, onto his trolley. The professor wondered how many Scotsmen had laid down their lives or at least their kilts for its creation.

"Let's go get a drink," she said once they finished checking in, "come on, come on, I won't eat you up." Professor Jayaweera picked up his small hold-all and followed her upstairs. At the bar a large caramel-coloured man materialised beside them.

"Say Hi to Vyvyan," she said. Vyvyan was smiling. He too was wearing a lot of gold, though mostly in the mouth. You could truly say his smile lit up the room, and the professor basked in its golden glow.

"Take good care of my friend's suitcase," he said, enveloping the professor's bony fingers in hands the size of dinner plates.

"There's nothing to take care of," the Professor assured him.

"No there isn't," said the woman, "I'll be clearing it at the other end, don't you worry 'bout a thing, I'll have a brandy and coke, that's what I'll have."

By the time the professor returned with the drinks Vyvyan had vanished.

"Cheers!" she said. The professor noted that, with her slanting blue headdress and the copper-coloured hollows in her cheeks, she had the sort of angular beauty you associated with ancient Egyptian queens. He began to see endless possibilities through the gap in her teeth.

"This your first visit?"

He nodded.

"Ah Miami!" she said. "It's the only place to be. I'm from San Juan myself, but business keeps me in Florida."

"I usually go to Sri Lanka for my holidays," Professor Jayaweera volunteered.

"Sierra Lanka? Isn't that somewhere in Africa?"

"You're thinking of Sierra Leone," he told her. But that didn't seem to ring a bell.

"Never mind," she said gaily, "let me show you round when we get there. I'll take you round in my silver grey BMW, that's what I'll do. You and I can have a great time, a *great* time."

The professor reflected that it wasn't his usual style, sitting in an airport bar drinking brandy and coke with a strange woman; but this was the summer of 1983 after all, and he was on his way to Miami.

"And the Keys…" she was saying. He had looked at pictures of the Keys before. Through the gap in her teeth he could see the thin grey concrete bridges shooting out to the horizon, straight and true, over clear green seas.

"Key West," he said excitedly, getting into the spirit of the thing, "we could go see Hemingway's house!"

"Who's Hemingway?" she asked suspiciously.

He opened his mouth to explain but she cut in. "Key West is for *hippy has-beens*," she said. "You need Isla Morada, that's what you need. You need to taste the Key Lime Pie at Manny and Isa's, that's what you need to taste."

And he could taste it already.

They got separated in the flight cabin. He could see her bright blue headdress bobbing about, a few rows up. The professor was used to the fourteen hour flight to Colombo, so eight hours to Miami was nothing. Once in the air, doubts began to assail him. What if the bag had gold in it? It had been awfully heavy. Explosives? Drugs? But then why would she pack it into such a spectacularly vulgar and noticeable bag? Because it's a double-bluff, he said to himself and it's checked through on your ticket. But *she* was clearing it at the other end. And if she's caught, he thought bitterly, she'll simply say she took it by mistake and point the finger at you.

The flight attendant gave them their landing cards. "No guns, no drugs, no explosives, no food, cooked or otherwise..." The list was endless. The plane dropped a few feet in the air and he felt sick in the pit of his stomach.

It was almost a relief therefore when he got a tap on the shoulder at Miami airport. "Would you like to step this way, please, sir? We'd like to ask you a few questions." The woman who led him away was decorated with truncheons and chains. There was a bunch of keys at her waist and what looked like handcuffs dangling from her hip-pocket. What's with you New World Women, he wanted to ask, all hung about with hardware? But the professor was not afraid: all his young life he had lived amongst women, his mother, his aunts, his grandmother. He knew women, he understood them and he loved them. Even in London where he lived alone they came to him like flies to honey. He looked at his interrogator with her freshly painted pink face and her fluffy golden hair: he thought of flap-jacks and maple syrup, of leaves turning red in the fall and bacon sizzling over woodsmoke, and he was not afraid.

She took him into a room partitioned off with glass and sat down with a great clashing of truncheons and crunching of chains. She began to rifle through his passport. The professor noticed that the glass walls of the room were reflective, so he could see out but nobody could see in. He watched a balding man artfully rearrange his hair only a few feet away from him on the other side of the glass. He wanted to tap on the glass and go "Shoo!"

"Will you pay attention, please, Sir?"

The professor looked up with regret.

"For what particular reason have you come to Miami?"

"For a holiday," he said surprised.

"I notice from your passport that you've only ever been in Sri Lanka and England. If you don't mind me saying so, we don't usually get many visitors from your part of the world."

"I'm a professor of English," he replied. "I've come to spend a holiday with a former pupil of mine." He told her all about Myra. "She'll be waiting outside if you want to speak to her."

"That will not be necessary, sir. Now, before I give you back your passport and allow you to walk through that door, is there anything you'd like to tell me, any piece of information you think might be helpful?"

The professor had a sudden urge to tell her everything. It was not his suitcase. He had not packed it. The truth was that he had wanted to be a good citizen, to be helpful.

He had acted within his own code of decency and good manners but it had been a mistake and he was sorry. She would understand. Of course she would. But he remembered in time that in the West the lines of justice ran straight and true, like arrows to the horizon. There was no room for the subtle feng-shui curves of human error.

She was looking at him now with the boiled-blue eyes of her witch-burning ancestors and he began to feel afraid. He took the passport from her and slowly got to his feet.

"I don't think so," he said softly.

"Y'all have a nice day," she replied.

Outside, all was quiet at the baggage carousel. There was a single battered suitcase going round and round in a desultory sort of way, like a lone nun on a merry-go-round. It was his. He heard the faint whirring of a luggage trolley at the other end of the hall and looked up in time to see a flash of blue disappearing round the corner.

There seemed to be no one about, not even at customs, when he wheeled his suitcase through.

Myra stood on tiptoe to give him a hug.

"Have you brought it?" she asked anxiously.

"Ssh!" he warned. "Later. They're watching us."

When they were safely out on the freeway she asked him again.

Without saying a word he opened the zip of his holdall and took out a brown paper bag, now soggy with steam. Inside were three *char-siu-paos* freshly steamed that morning back in Soho, London. He took one out, broke it, and popped half into her mouth.

"Oh Professor," she breathed, "you doll!"

He began to eat the other half, the red, caramelised pork in its steamed white dough, the very definition of heaven. Just then a car drew up by them in the next lane, a silver grey BMW. For a moment there he was suspended, motionless between the two women, and he felt strangely comforted. He turned towards the familiar blue turban and smiled, a ghastly smile stained red with flecks of caramelised meat, but she looked at him contemptuously and looked away. There was not even a flicker of recognition in her eyes.

Then, with a sudden surge of speed, the BMW shot past, straight and true, like an arrow to the horizon.

A Few Days After Eleven

John-John's father woke him up one black morning in the Horn of Africa, a few days after eleven. "Time to go," he said.

John-John's mother was away at his grandfather's funeral, so John-John had done all the packing himself. He put the last bits in, his pyjamas, his toothbrush. In those days the only way out of Mogadiscio was on Alitalia, via Addis and Asmara to Rome. Then onwards to boarding school in England.

The airport was a single storey building surrounded by a cattle-grid, with mosquito netting in the windows. It looked like somebody's Granny's retirement bungalow, though your average Granny would probably not have had the cattle-grid.

John-John's father took him up the gangway and sat him down in the plane. He squeezed his shoulder and was gone. A kiss would have been nice, John-John thought wistfully, these Kandyan fathers they're so derelict in their duties.

When the plane was up in the air, the passengers began to talk and smoke. The atmosphere was foggier inside than out, and the air-hostess tap-tapped her way through the haze in the cabin. She could have done with a white stick, John-John thought. The Italians talked till you were blue in the face, then they smoked at you, then they talked some more. Those were the days when talking and smoking were *the* Italian national pastimes.

When John-John reached for the sick bag the third time, though, there was a momentary hush. Sri Lanka one, Italy nil, he thought victoriously.

But the Italians struck back at lunch: liver: the great equalizer. Those were the days an airline could serve you liver for lunch and get away with it. John-John left it untouched. His sick bag was full anyway.

In Asmara somebody was checking in a large black dog they had bought a ticket for. Those days you could do things like that. There was a painted woman at the duty-free standing motionless against the plate glass, with the brown Asmara hills beyond. Her face was painted pink and her eyes were painted blue and her hair was painted black. There was a faint tinkle from her chandelier earrings when they caught the breeze from the air-conditioner.

At Rome they handed him over to a universal Aunt in a short blue skirt. Her duties did not extend to carrying his suitcase, so she strode ahead, and it was all John-John could do to keep up. In those days there were no baggage trolleys. They walked and walked, the airport was endless. It took so long to reach their destination, he thought she must surely be a grand-aunt by now.

They took a coach and it was night by the time they reached the hotel. She handed him over to the man behind the desk who was very loving towards her. Maybe she's his universal Aunt too, John-John thought, he's hugging her so much.

John-John unpacked his toothbrush and his pyjamas. He got into bed but didn't dare go to sleep because he had to be up by 4.30 next morning and he did not have an alarm clock. I should not have to be doing all this at my age, he thought, I'm only a few days after eleven.

In between snatches of wakefulness he dreamt of Africa, of eating devilled chicken with his fingers at Afgoi, while his parents danced under the green neon lights in the garden.

At 4.30 sharp he heaved his suitcase down the stairs. It slipped down the last flight, landing at the bottom with a crash. The noise woke up the universal nephew behind the desk who went out and woke up the coach driver who drove John-John back to the airport.

He arrived in London as a misty green dawn was breaking. Uncle David met him at Heathrow. He wasn't his real uncle, only a friend of John-John's father, who worked for the British Council.

"It's all right Harry, he's one of mine," he said to the man at Immigration and walked John-John straight through. In those days you could do things like that.

Uncle David wore a hearing aid and spoke in a singsong voice.

"You've arrived far too early," he complained.

I know that, John-John wanted to reply, I'm only a few days after eleven.

Back at the flat at Osnaburgh Street Uncle David showed him how he was going to put two armchairs together to make up his bed for the night.

He switched on the TV. A very beautiful girl with a mole on her face was playing the guitar and singing.

She was singing in black and white.

She sang:

"Those were the days, my friend,
We thought they'd never end..."

But John-John was rather afraid they had. Somewhere back there on a plane, high up in the air between Asmara and Rome.

Ice Cream Karma

They had everything in common, they had nothing in common, the two women seated side by side in the half-empty plane in their kaftans and mirrored glasses. Mrs. Herath lived in a council flat in Stockwell, so cutting-edge, so *dangerous*! Mrs. Sarath resided in charming Chislehurst, so suburban, so *chic*! But Abroad is the great leveller, and to the native Sri Lankan eye they were virtually identical, down to the SARS masks both were wearing.

Mrs. Herath and Mrs. Sarath were taking the cheap flight to Colombo, through SARS-struck Singapore. They hardly spoke to each other - indeed the masks made conversation virtually impossible - and to the stewardess not at all. At Singapore, waiting for their connection, they wandered around the airport sticking close to each other in the hope that their combined non-SARS aura might ward off any evil in the air.

"My husband is already in Sri Lanka," confided Mrs. Herath, as if it were some dirty secret.

"My husband is in heaven," tittered Mrs. Sarath. Her husband, T.K. Sarath, had been cook at the Ceylon Students Centre in London, way back in the Seventies. Two months before his visa ran out he had vanished into the hinterland, made his money on a string of Balti Houses, and ended up in charming Chislehurst, dying quite soon thereafter. Somewhere along the way he had acquired Mrs. T.K. Sarath, who furthered the meteoric rise of the Sarath star, plunging her curry-money recklessly into charitable works. Karma had been good to her, and she was determined to be good back. Indeed there wasn't a single poor man in Chislehurst who hadn't suffered from her ministrations.

Mrs. Herath had been born to a Kandyan *walauwa*, with all that that entailed, though there was not much evidence of it in the council flat in Stockwell, where the graffiti-daubed staircases smelt of urine and well-matured dog turd. In the evenings there was the music of breaking glass to soothe the savage breast.

Back in Colombo Mrs. Herath might have been thought to have the edge, however slight, over Mrs. Sarath, but Abroad is like a great washing machine Out There, spinning you out of your karmic cycle and washing you clean of any iconographic associations your name might have: all you could see now were two old biddies in kaftans and mirrored glasses, walking slowly through a deserted Colombo airport.

At Customs they caused a minor panic by whipping off their masks.

"That's better! This Colombo air is so clammy."

"Are you going through red or green?"

"I always go through red," said Mrs. Sarath, "I have *so* many things to declare." She bought an entirely new wardrobe each time she came out, and would have dearly loved to declare each and every item in detail.

"What's this?" asked the customs officer.

"That's an original Ralph Lauren polo shirt. I bought it in Oxford Street."

"Oxford?" The officer looked at her in disbelief. "You mean Piliyandala!"

He waved her through. "And what have *you* got to declare?" he asked the next lady.

"Only my SARS, I'm afraid," said Mrs. Herath quite loudly. She was bundled through double-quick.

They shared a van into Colombo.

"My husband was too busy to come to the airport," explained Mrs. Herath.

"He's planting sweet potatoes today, the old goat."

Mrs. Sarath did not comment. If she thought it odd that Mr. Herath preferred potatoes to Mrs Herath, she did not say. The truth was that after thirty years of marriage the

Heraths had arrived at a satisfactory working relationship. They shot back and forth between Stockwell in London and the little bungalow they had bought at retirement in Deal Place, Colpetty, but never together, never in unison: when one was *to-ing*, the other was frequently to be found *fro-ing*, and it so happened that they were never under the same roof for any great length of time. In fact there had been that glorious moment last year when they met outside Colombo airport for all of five minutes, their opposing trolleys nudging each other in a hurry to get a move on.

At Deal Place Mrs. Sarath came in for a cup of tea.

"Welcome home, my dear," said Mr. Herath to Mrs. Herath. He seemed genuinely glad to see her. He was a tall reddish man with curly grey hair and huge hands.

"Janaka, I'd like you to meet my friend Mrs. Sarath."

"Oh, call me Dhania," tittered Mrs. Sarath, visibly moved. "Upali!" shouted Mr. Herath. "Upalee…!" He turned to his wife. "You should see the help Malice has found for us this time."

"Malice?" said his wife. "Don't be wicked, Janaka. What *will* Dhania think? Alice is my sister-in-law," she explained to Mrs. Sarath. "She lives up in Kandy at the *Walauwa*, my ancestral home. She has my power of attorney and manages all our affairs while we're abroad. Actually, I don't know how we'd manage without her. She even finds us staff."

"Not that they ever last very long," added Mr. Herath, with a meaningful look at his wife.

"I don't know how it is," continued Mrs. Herath ignoring him, "I manage perfectly well back in London

without any help at all. But out here I just go to pieces.
I can't seem to do a thing for myself - I have to have
someone there to help me."

At that moment there was an apparition at the
doorway. It was tall and slim and good-looking. It wore
bright orange sneakers and those very long shorts that reach
almost down to ankle level and flap helplessly at that point.
There were many and various multicoloured layers on top.
All in all, it looked like a newly rescued boat person,
perhaps, fresh off the high seas after an abortive attempt at
entry into Italy.

"Ah Upali," said Mr. Herath, "make us some tea, like a
good boy."

Mrs. Herath and Mrs. Sarath stood there gobsmacked.

The tea duly arrived in three assorted cups, the frothy
boiled milk forming a scum on the surface of the cup, the
saucer, the tray, and finally on the expensive Sarath lap.

"My cup runneth over," said Mr. Herath jovially,
"nothing like good *kadé* tea, no?" He slurped noisily.

Mrs. Sarath said nothing. In charming Chislehurst she
drank only Lapsang Souchong or Lady Londonderry. She
was quite prepared to slum it with PG tips, for she knew in
her heart she was a brave woman, but nothing had prepared
her for this.

"Take it away!" roared Mrs. Herath who had got her
voice back. "Never, *never* boil the milk, and always, *always*,
serve it separately. And make sure the cups match next
time!"

❄ ❄ ❄

And so the battle lines were drawn within five minutes of Mrs. Herath entering the house. Upali went into the kitchen and had a quiet fit in there, all by himself. He blamed it all on that bitch up at the walauwa, the *Kumarihamy,* who had fixed him up in this job after interviewing him and his father.

"Mrs. Herath, my sister-in-law, can be *quite* difficult at times," she had said. "Nobody knows this better than I do." She paused for effect. "But you will, after all, be very well paid. For fifteen thousand rupees a month I am sure you can put up with anything."

Upali's father looked at him in wonderment. So what if his son was being asked to be a domestic? Fifteen thousand a month was more than a state employee earned in a Government office, and would go a long way towards the new roof on their house. They were replacing the thatch with tiles and this sudden summons to the walauwa with the promise of a job offer seemed to the old man like a summons from heaven.

They were seated on the front veranda of the walauwa, a rare honour. The families of the old man and the Kumarihamy had been allied in marriage some hundred odd years back. At that time, the old man's family had been every bit as good as the Kumarihamy's. But the fifty-two flavours, the iridescent ice cream colours of karma had been terribly unkind, and four generations later all that was left to him was the seven acres of paddy land and the *Bandara* to the end of his name. But the same karma had been deliciously kind to the Kumarihamy: a brilliant marriage to Mrs. Herath's brother had brought her the title as well as his ancestral house, the walauwa, a pocket palazzo sitting atop a hill overlooking the Kandy Lake. But the ties of kinship between the old man's family and the Kumarihamy's ran inexorably on, an invisible underground stream unseen by anyone and rarely mentioned in public, except when it bubbled up unexpectedly to the surface every now and then. It was bubbling now, at the Kumarihamy's command; hence the seat on the front verandah for Upali and his father, as opposed to the bench round the back in the kitchens, which would normally have been their lot.

"There is, however, one thing I would ask of you, my commission so to speak, for having found you this job," said the Kumarihamy. The old man and his son shifted uneasily on their seats.

"I would ask you to keep me informed of their movements, the comings and goings in the Herath household. You can call me here at the walauwa day or night."

"I wonder what the old bitch has up her sleeve," muttered the old man to Upali as they descended the rock-cut steps to the walauwa gates and the bus back home. There was no love lost between the two families, the greed of the one and the envy of the other being too much for each to handle, but money was money, and the lure of a new roof was too thrilling to ignore.

It was soon after Mrs. Herath joined Mr. Herath at Deal Place that Popeye arrived. He came by air, as Sri Lankan dogs often do, having been thrown over the garden wall by the neighbours at the back. Mr. Herath found him scrabbling about in his sweet potato patch early one morning, a yellow wire-haired mongrel with a strong dash of Cairn terrier in him. He had a pronounced tufted beard which brought out all Mrs. Herath's hairdressing instincts - she had qualified in London years ago but never practised - and Mr. Herath had to be very firm with her and lock up the scissors.

"We can't keep him," said Mr. Herath, "he'll ruin my sweet potatoes."

Mrs. Herath looked pleadingly at him.

Popeye looked pleadingly at him.

"Oh all *right*," said Mr. Herath, "but only if the people at the back don't want him."

So they carried him round to the house at the back and rang the doorbell.

"Yes?" said the woman who opened the door. Popeye began to growl at her and she took a step back. "No," she continued, as if they had asked her a question, "I've never seen this dog before in my *life*." She slammed the door on them.

"Well that's that, then," said Mr. Herath.

"Charming," said Mrs. Herath.

And so Popeye settled in, and with true canine instincts transferred his affections within days of arriving to the one person that mattered: the one who fed him: Upali. Never mind all the love and affection Mr. and Mrs. Herath showered on him, the diamanté dog collars and fancy foreign shampoos, the meaty morsels from Colpetty Market and the expensive visits to Ching the vet. Popeye followed Upali around everywhere and took up residence in his room, frequently growling at Mrs. Herath when he caught her snooping in there.

Upali for his part would have happily thrown the dog back, with his sublime Sri Lankan instincts of non-violence, but there was no guarantee the matter would end there, and he was not about to start a game of doggie ping-pong with the neighbour over the garden wall.

❀   ❀   ❀

"Upalee! Upalee…!" The cry cut through the mists of Upali's consciousness as he rolled over in his comfortable bed. Every morning his employer marched into his room with scant regard for his modesty, drawing back the curtains, whipping back the bedclothes. Really, the shamelessness of these Returnees!

Every morning, in those two delicious minutes between sleep and wakefulness, with the banshee wail of "Upalee!" in the background, Upali repeated this mantra to himself: I do not *hav*e to be here, I do *not* have to be here, *I* do not have to be here. I am only here because this is an adventure for me, the bright lights, the big city, and I am bored *shitless* back home in the village. The thatched roof has nothing to do with it. I will up and go the *minute* I get fed up, and my father can bugger off.

His employers made Upali's life very comfortable indeed: there was a mosquito net over the bed, a fan on the ceiling and even a strip of carpet by the bed, all things unheard of back home in the village.

"We must make sure he understands that we believe in the Dignity of Human Labour," said Mrs. Herath to her husband. At times like these she liked to speak in capitals.

"Not the way *some people* treat their staff." The staff at the walauwa were paid next to nothing, and treated like serfs in pre-revolutionary Russia, the Kumarihamy ruling over them with an iron hand. Strangely, they stayed on and on, while the Heraths found it difficult to keep anyone for more than a few months at a time.

Mrs. Herath paid handsomely, but expected value for money. For his fifteen thousand, Upali was expected to cook, clean, look after the dog and do the odd bit of gardening, such as helping out Mr. Herath with his sweet potatoes. For his pains he got every afternoon off between five and seven, and Sundays and Poya days. Upali understood English perfectly but preferred not to, managing only with the words 'yes' and 'no', and held this pretended ignorance like a great Sinhala sword over his employers. Anything he didn't want to do he didn't do, and he had wonderful reasons why not. Thirty years in Stockwell had wreaked havoc on Mrs. Herath's Sinhalese, and all she could do was nod and try vainly to follow the intricacies of his arcane reasoning. Who knows how far Upali might have gone with a good solid education behind him? He might have become a politician. Or even a con-artist.

Every morning she went through her check-list with him:

"Have you made the beds?"   "Yes."

"Have you swept the stairs?"   "Yes."

"Have you de-ticked the dog?"   "Yes."

"Have you done the bathrooms?"   "No."

"Why not?"   "No Vim."

That phrase 'no Vim' was the jewel in his English crown, and he worked on it assiduously, polishing it up like some rare gem in the privacy of his bedroom.

"Well go and bloody get some!" roared Mrs. Herath irritably. She was in a sad bad mood that morning.

Virtually every day Upali went off to Rahumania's the corner shop with a list.

"Chilli, garlic, coconuts and two chickens," wrote Mrs. Herath. "And tell them to give you some *decent* chickens, not like those crows you came back with the other day."

Upali loved these outings. He had introduced a discreet system of wealth tax on the Heraths: it was an easy matter to get the girl at Rahumania's to increase the price of each item on the handwritten bill by a few rupees, not much, but enough to keep him in daily soft drinks.

"Now go!" said Mrs. Herath. She was in a hurry because Mrs. Sarath was expected that morning. The two ladies were planning a tour of the country - "to *really* see it, dear, like the natives do" - and there was a lot of planning ahead.

Upali hung about uncertainly.

"*Go, go, go!*" bellowed Mrs. Herath. She might have been a rugby coach.

Upali scarpered.

❈ ❈ ❈

"Come in, come in," said Mr. Herath to Mrs. Sarath. "My wife is in one of her moods this morning. She always gets like this after about a week here. If you're not careful she'll tell you the Sad Story of her Life."

Now the Sad Story of Mrs. Herath's Life did not really have anything to do with Mr. Herath, as might be imagined. Mr. Herath was an *addendum*, a postscript merely, to its Sadness. It was to do with the fifty odd acres of Jackwood plantation that Mrs. Herath's father did not leave her in his will. Mrs. Herath's father had not spoken to her for about thirty years before his death, having cut her off without a cent when she married dear, unsuitable Mr. Herath. After marriage the couple had run off to England in a huff and all contact with her family had ceased.

Although she had not spoken to her father before his death, she knew in her heart of hearts that he wanted her to have the *Coswatte*, as it was called, but there was no way of proving it. It had gone, together with the other estates of the walauwa to her brother. Her brother had agreed with her in principle that the Coswatte should come to her, but he too had died without doing anything about it, and everything was now in the Kumarihamy's capable hands. Things were further complicated by the Land Reform Commission, which had subsequently vested the Coswatte in the government. The statute of limitations on an appeal had run out before Mrs. Herath woke up to the fact, and the Kumarihamy was now dealing with various government departments on her behalf.

"You're never really here long enough to follow it through," the Kumarihamy reproved her gently. "Besides, what will you do if you get it?"

"Nothing particularly," Mrs. Herath replied. "It's the principle of the thing. I know he wanted me to have it, and I'll be damned if I let the government enjoy it."

"Maybe we could grow sweet potatoes on it," suggested Mr. Herath jovially.

The Kumarihamy shuddered. She knew better than anyone that you can't mess like that with your karma, which is like ice-cream on the tip of your tongue: gone before you know it if you're not careful. And the Heraths were not careful people.

❋   ❋   ❋

Mrs. Sarath was dressed from head to toe in designer wear. It was nine-thirty in the morning and she was fully made up, her face giving off a strange grey gleam in the cruel tropical light. She had rented the penthouse suite at Crescat for a month and she felt she owed it to her position as the most expensive tenant in the building to be perfectly turned out. So it was not for her arrival at Deal Place that she had dressed, but rather, for her departure from Crescat.

She wore a brand new bright orange polo shirt with the words Ralph Lauren on it. Underneath was the familiar embroidered logo of a polo player on a horse.

"Even my knickers are new," she whispered to Mrs. Herath conspiratorially, "M. & S, from Oxford Street. Sometimes, when I am dressed all new like this, I feel like a new woman."

"Sometimes, so do I," added Mr. Herath, to no one in particular.

They heard the key in the front door and Upali entered. He hovered behind Mrs. Sarath's chair laden with various plastic bags. He was dressed in an identical bright orange polo shirt.

"Get out!" roared Mrs. Herath, but it was too late. Mrs. Sarath turned around, saw, and was not happy.

"Come over here," she beckoned with her finger.

Upali approached shyly. "Only two hundred rupees in Piliyandala," he said, in a sudden alarming burst of fluency.

His shirt had the words Ralph Lorensz on it. Underneath was the familiar embroidered logo of a man in a three-wheeler. ·

Mrs. Sarath's brow cleared. "See!" she said, "I told you it wasn't the same. I paid *forty pounds* for mine in Selfridges." She shivered slightly, as if she had just come in from the rain.

Mrs. Herath felt it was time to change the subject.

"Let me tell you the Sad Story of my Life," she began, and everyone immediately stopped listening. "So that is why, dear Dhania," she concluded some twenty minutes later, "when we're on our trip, we must stop at the Coswatte first, *before* we get to the walauwa."

❀　❀　❀

And so the days rolled by, with Mr. Herath cultivating his sweet potatoes and Upali quietly taking over the running of the house. He was becoming quite a good cook, wielding his meat cleaver on the Rahumania chickens like a Chinese film star. Mrs. Herath for her part would have preferred her chickens boneless from Sainsburys with their little accompanying sachets of Kung Pao sauce, but she was willing to put up with real home cooking for a change. This was, after all, the Third World.

Upali's employers drove him nuts with their unreasonable demands, and some days he could happily have murdered them. They wanted everything picture-perfect, the way it never was in England, the way it never would be in Deal Place, not with Upali at the helm.

Popeye followed him around slavishly. Somewhere in the fog of his doggy brain he probably realised that by flying over the garden wall he had landed feet first on the great ice cream swirl patterns of the Herath karma.

Mrs. Herath and Mrs. Sarath hired themselves a van for their forthcoming trip.

"AC or non-AC?"

"I think non-AC, dear," said Mrs. Sarath. "After all, we *do* want to experience the country like the natives." But she was thinking of Chislehurst as she said this.

Mrs. Herath did not think of her flat in Stockwell. There was not much there worth thinking about.

Of the two ladies, Mrs. Sarath was Upali's favourite, his secret pin-up girl, his Miss Abroad 2003. He envied her her coats of many colours and her abundance of labels, her dazzling *returnee chic*. His best friend had once gone abroad, but had returned almost immediately, scandalised by the notion that over there they expected you to *work* for your money. So Upali knew he had to be content with Colpetty instead, and content he was.

The neighbourhood of Deal Place was what was called a mixed residential area, with houses as well as shops and offices: there was Sivapalan's Tutory, favoured by pretty young girls in hipster jeans; there was old Madam Amaravati who taught singing and could be heard warbling in a thin cracked voice through the twilight hours; then there was the young bloke with the coloured red hair in the computer shop who batted his eyelashes meaningfully each time Upali went past; and there was Miss Oorloff, who gave French lessons in an upstairs room (discipline was strict). But Upali's all time favourite was the Matara Tea Rooms, an enterprise, run from a corrugated zinc shack set up in a vacant lot, which the absentee landlords had been trying vainly for years to evict. There were three iron tables set up under the banana trees, and various logs on which patrons sat. Nobody was fussy: they were not there for the food, they were there for the ambience.

Every afternoon at five Upali stepped out, razor sharp in his Bandara Nike Air trainers, his Colvin R. Klein boxers with the waistband showing (important that) and his Dolce & Gampaha tee shirt.

"There goes Piliyandala Man," said Mr. Herath, but Upali did not hear. He was in heaven.

He went to the Matara Tea Rooms and flung himself onto a chair, putting his feet up on another.

"Aney nangi," he would say, *"api cool ekak bomu the*?" - Hey little sister, how about a cool one? - but so much more chic, so much more cutting edge in the vernacular. This was the Time, this was the Place. This was his karma in the Here and Now. Not under some thatched roof back in the village.

❄   ❄   ❄

The two returnees finally set off on their travels. Mr. Herath declined to join, having organised a trip of his own with his golfing buddies, and Upali was left in sole charge. He immediately called up the walauwa with details of the various itineraries.

Mrs. Herath and Mrs. Sarath stopped at three temples along the Kandy Road.

"Don't you find, dear, that once you've seen one temple you've seen the lot?" asked Mrs. Herath.

"In Chislehurst we don't *have* temples," added Mrs. Sarath, a little unnecessarily.

They visited the Coswatte, and arrived finally at the walauwa gates.

"This is as far as we go," explained Mrs. Herath. "From here upwards we walk.

In the old days," she said, "they were carried up in litters."

Mrs. Sarath looked incredulous. "You mean we can't drive up to the front door?"

It was all highly irregular, and not at all what she had been led to expect.

Standing in the late afternoon sunlight in her shapeless white cotton sari, the little Kumarihamy watched her belated lunch guests struggle up the steep stone-cut steps. Behind her the house brooded like a frog on a rock. What an ungainly woman her sister-in-law was, with her large hands and feet, so gauche, so *un-Kandyan*! Each time she returned from England she seemed to have grown that much bigger! The Kumarihamy sighed with pleasure as she looked down at her own exquisite toes, now wriggling in their unfamiliar rubber slippers.

"Alice!" panted Mrs. Herath, "meet my friend Dhania. Dhania, Alice."

"You can call me Kumarihamy," said the Kumarihamy.

"Committee Mary? What a charming name!"

The Kumarihamy gave up and led them into the house, leaving her slippers ostentatiously on the verandah and walking in barefoot. The others, unsure of what to do, did not follow suit.

Mrs. Herath was plunged immediately into the comforting damp smells of childhood.

Mrs. Sarath saw only the blued *chunam* walls, the little pink and green squares of pre-war frosted glass, the hopelessly uneven cement floors. They had not warned her about all this in Chislehurst.

Almost immediately, they were served three full glasses of water. Mrs. Herath and the Kumarihamy touched theirs. Mrs. Sarath drank hers in one gulp.

"You're not supposed to drink it," chided the Kumarihamy gently, "it is a symbolic way of saying 'lunch is served.' We here in Kandy try to follow the traditions of our forefathers in everything, the age-old tried and tested ways of doing things. For instance, we speak Sinhala Only, in this house." She paused. "Of course, we do make exceptions, for people like you who would find that difficult."

"How wonderful, Karate Mummy, how *ethnic*!"

Mrs. Herath silently noted how her sister-in-law liked to use her title at every possible occasion. She thought back with a little stab of nostalgia to the days of her mother, the old Kumarihamy, who had been impossibly grand, and who almost *never* used her title, expecting people to know instead who she was. Back then English was spoken in the house. Sinhala Only was for backwoods aristocrats who chewed betel and kept chickens.

They sat down to lunch, the guests noting with dismay that there was no cutlery on the table.

"Sita!" shouted the Kumarihamy, "Sita!" She rang a little bell. Sita brought in some assorted kitchen cutlery, a spoon and fork for Mrs. Herath, a spoon only for Mrs. Sarath. The Kumarihamy ate with her fingers. Mrs. Herath idly wondered what had happened to all the old English silver.

"We visited the Coswatte," she said. "What is the latest on that, Alice?"

The Kumarihamy shook her head. "Not much change, I'm afraid. I've been to the Land Reform Commission half a dozen times in the last few months." She turned to Mrs. Sarath. "The problem with this country is that each time the government changes you get a new set of officials in each department, and you have to start at the bottom all over again to get anything done."

"Tell me about it, Mata Hari, tell me about it!"

What the Kumarihamy did not add was that lying at the bottom of her almirah was a letter from the LRC which had arrived two weeks ago, granting the Coswatte back to its original owner. It was addressed to Mrs. Herath's father because the LRC records dated from before his death. The Kumarihamy was waiting patiently till the returnees returned, to take possession. There was no need for them to know, and with luck they need never know.

Now the Kumarihamy was not by nature a wicked woman. But she felt that wickedness was *incumbent* upon her position as chatelaine of the walauwa and all its estates: her entire karma, it seemed to her, was *permeated* by the rum-and-raisin flavours of wickedness.

If the Heraths ever got their hands on the property they would begin by cutting down all the jack trees for seed money. Then would come some damned fool project or other, guaranteed to lose money in spectacular fashion; after that, the indignity of Mr. Herath's sweet potatoes; and then the final outrage, the sale to a developer for housing. The Kumarihamy could see it all, with the blinding clarity of a prophetess: at times she felt like the woman who sold the ice creams in the karma shop.

So instead, she kept quiet about the letter, and watched with sly amusement as her lunch guests attempted to tackle their curried drumsticks with spoons and forks. After a while she asked: "How is Upali?"

"Settling in very well," said Mrs. Herath, "settling in very well. In fact I've grown quite fond of the boy. I do hope he'll last."

With lunch over, the guests were keen to be off. They were on their way to Nuwara Eliya, which Mrs. Sarath felt sure would turn out to be her spiritual home in Sri Lanka: a sort of Chislehurst-up-there-in-the-Hills.

"That was wonderful, Rummy Tatami, just wonderful."

"Oh it was nothing," said the Kumarihamy waving her hand airily. A pink ray of light off the window glass caught the cabochon ruby on her finger, and she put her hand down quickly. The ring had belonged to her mother-in-law.

She watched her guests depart with relief. She felt sorry for these returnees, blundering back and forth between continents, but these yearly visits were a severe trial to her. If only they could be persuaded to return less often!

"Somebody told me I should speak to the Minister directly," said Mrs. Herath as she kissed her sister-in-law goodbye. "One word from him, apparently, and the Coswatte would be returned to me immediately."

"You do that," said the Kumarihamy. If she felt alarmed or threatened in any way she did not show it, because she knew how absurdly easy it was for her to send the Heraths packing, to bring down the house of cards in Deal Place. She had done it many times before.

She waited for her guests to go, and made a single phone call.

It was late. Shrugging off her shapeless sari with distaste, the little Kumarihamy ran her bath. She opened her almirah, the one that contained the fateful letter, and took from it the little black beaded dress, the pointed Prada shoes. These were not from Piliyandala, alas, or even Oxford Street. They were from Milan. To go round her neck she chose a heavy piece of Kandyan jewellery, barbaric in splendour, quite the best that karma could buy. That evening she was meeting a few select girlfriends for drinks and dancing at *Le Garage*. While she went happily back and forth between bedroom and bathroom she sang:

"Karma, karma, karma, karma, karma chameleon ..."

❋   ❋   ❋

Upali's hand was shaking when he put the phone down. The Kumarihamy had been brutally succinct.

"They had nothing but contempt for you," she said. "They spent the entire meal laughing at you, your clothes, your behaviour. But mostly they made fun of your English, and that I find absolutely inexcusable. Because of my relationship with your father, however distant, I have taken all this as a *personal* insult. I therefore give you full permission to leave immediately. You don't have to wait a moment longer. I will immediately send a full month's salary to your father."

But Upali did not go. With her long-handled silver spoon the Kumarihamy had simply reached out and stirred up that little sediment of madness that lies at the bottom of every good Sri Lankan brain. It was so easy to do, it was what every politician did at election time. So Upali was not ready to go, not by a long shot. No way, *not yet.*

The old biddies were coming back today, and they had called ahead to order dinner because they would be late getting in.

"Two chickens from Rahumania, and for God's sake make sure they're fleshy!"

Mr. Herath was also expected back, any moment now, in fact.

There had been an awful mess in the kitchen but Upali had cleaned it all up. He took the curry off the stove and put it on the electric hotplate in the dining room where it bubbled gently, in readiness for the guests.

Upali's few belongings were packed. He left the house, slamming the door shut and throwing his key carelessly into a flowerbed. This little act gave him a great sense of freedom and empowerment. He headed off to his date with karma at the Matara Tea Rooms, like a cowboy riding into a vanilla sunset.

Mr. Herath returned to an empty house, no Upali, no Popeye. 'Boys will be boys and dogs will be dogs,' he thought. He spent a happy hour alone among his potatoes.

The two ladies arrived much later, after dark. Absolutely no housework seemed to have been done in their absence, but what the hell, it was good to be home.

Everyone agreed that the dinner was sensational.

"I have never eaten such a chicken," said Mrs. Sarath, "not even in Chislehurst."

Next morning Mrs. Herath got up late. Her husband was already out in the garden, harvesting potatoes.

"Upalee! Upalee!" She burst into Upali's room but it was empty.

She made herself a cup of coffee and went outside to watch her husband.

"A really good crop this time, my dear," he said, "I do believe I've surpassed myself. Just look at this one, a real *whopper*!"

He raised the spade. On it was the unmistakeable head, the yellow hair, the tufted beard.

Mrs. Herath watched in horror.

"Funny thing," said Mr. Herath digging further, "the rest of him seems to be missing."

Patas! With a small explosion the truth scorched Mrs. Herath's brain: the missing boy, the missing dog, the sensational curry.

She ran retching to the bathroom.

"If you want to get ahead, get a dog!" said Mr. Herath jovially.

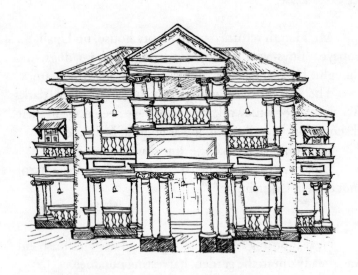

Agnes of God

The baby was just eight weeks old when Aunty Sweena rang.

"I have Agnes of God here for you."

"I beg your pardon?"

"You heard. Agnes of God. The nanny."

"But..."

"Are you coming to get her or not?" She could picture me, sitting up in bed with my afternoon tea, the hot little plate of breadfruit chips by my side, and she decided to go on the attack.

"I've been ringing you since two. Why don't you people ever pick up the phone?"

"Because..." *Because between two and four we knock the phone off so we can get a decent after-lunch nap.*

"Well?"

Well, I left the tea, I left the chips, I went for Agnes. I had visions of a virginal girl in a brown pinafore, St. Theresa the Little Flower perhaps, or Bernadette. Instead there was this middle-aged woman, nut brown, with straggling gray hair and shrewd eyes. But it was the teeth that struck you first: teeth that flew out at you like bats out of the mouth of a cave, almost parallel to the ground, low and welcoming.

"Mango-sucking teeth," said Sweena, by way of explanation.

My wife Devi and I looked in dismay. Out here in Sri Lanka there is a theory that your child's nanny must above all be nice-featured, so that your child's expressions will be sweet-tempered and calm in imitation.

We hesitated. Sweena drove the point of the dagger home: " I have at least two other people who will have her in a trice if you don't." Nannies, as you can gather, are thin on the ground here in Colombo.

"We'll take her," we said weakly.

"A thousand a month plus food," shot back Sweena. At this point Agnes herself piped up:

"I have to go home for the Sinhalese New Year."

"What New Year for you?!" said Sweena. "You're a Catholic. You'll get a week at Christmas and the long weekend at Easter." We bundled her into the car and brought her home.

And so ended an eight week nightmare.

When Devi first found out she was pregnant she told all her friends: "We're going to manage without a nanny. We want to instil our own proper values into this child, not somebody else's half-baked notions." Our friends looked concerned. Mostly from an aesthetic point of view, I fear. A nanny out here is the ultimate fashion accessory: you don't leave home without one. Devi's friend Avril, for instance, got herself not one but *two* nannies about six months before her happy event. She can be found any morning wandering around Odel's with one nanny carrying her cell phone and the other her shopping basket.

When they all saw Agnes their concern turned to visible distress, because fashion accessory she was not. But we were beyond caring. Devi was elbow deep in soiled nappies and I was to be found at all hours of the night walking up and down, up and down the verandah, while the baby practised scales. He was particularly good in C sharp minor. It got so bad that the proprietor of the Saivar Kadé, the caff across the road, sent us a stern message:

"Don't you know that it is very bad to make a *boy* child cry?"

"I'll make *him* cry if he doesn't get off my case," Devi muttered murderously. So you can imagine our relief when we drove Agnes in through the gates.

✳   ✳   ✳

People who see this house, with its long white columns and endless verandahs, immediately think, Colonial heaven: wooden ceiling fans and cocktails on the terrace served by barefoot native bearers in white jackets. Nothing could be further from the truth I assure you. There's the two of us rattling around in this enormous shell, and then there's Themis, old and lame and evil-tempered. The day Themis serves pink gins on the verandah I'll dance naked on the rooftops.

Of course there is plenty of other life in the house too, apart from Themis: there are rats and polecats, and we even have a pair of snakes, though I have only ever seen one: a six-foot-long *garandia,* a sort of harmless (*harmless?*) constrictor that swallows rats whole. We also have three dogs, though they don't count as they are thoroughly domesticated unlike Themis. We were not yet sure to which category Agnes belonged.

The servants quarters at the back are over a hundred foot long and Agnes had nine rooms to choose from. She chose the one furthest from Themis, wise woman.

"I don't eat pork or beef," she said, laying down the ground rules, "Nor squid nor crab. And please," she said earnestly, "chicken only occasionally."

"Well you'd better get into the kitchen with Themis then," said Devi briskly. "At least that way you'll be sure to get *something* to eat."

And so it turned out that though she came to look after the baby, Agnes began to spend more and more time in the kitchen, and the food coming out of there took a sharp turn for the better. At these times the baby went back to Devi. This is what always tends to happen. My old grandmother used to say: you get these servants, you end up doing their work for them.

Not that Agnes neglected the baby, for whom she had her own strange rules. At feeding time she would fly around the house with him in one hand and the food in the other. She would be back in five minutes flat.

"Finished, finished," she would say. "He's eaten everything."

"She's finishing it all herself," Devi would mutter. But we didn't dare investigate further: in a Nanny State you don't, do you?

To bathe the baby, she would squat in our shower tray with the baby on her knees and pour a hundred cups of water - it had to be a hundred, don't ask why - over his hollering head. As a result, to this day he can't stand getting his head wet and will spend all his time in the shower wriggling and dodging the downward stream of water.

Agnes was married to a tapper on Sweena's rubber estate in Kalutara. The husband was a drunk, as is quite common on these estates. Agnes and her husband lived in a line-room - a long narrow cabin partitioned into sections for each worker. As far as I could gather, conditions were as appalling and life as jolly as at any British Public School. They lived in and out of each other's pockets. They fought, they made up, and they fought again. Agnes had a daughter who was in service herself elsewhere in Colombo. As time went on, her husband's drinking got worse, and he began to beat her up. When Sweena got to hear, she made her estate conductor put Agnes on the first bus to Colombo, and here she was with us, though I couldn't help feeling she sometimes missed the abusive familiarity of the line-room. Here she only had Themis to fight with, and though he gamely put up a show he was no match for her. He would quietly come and sneak to us:

"Do you realize that woman is completely mad?"

"How do you mean?"

"She talks to herself."

"Well, so do you, Themis."

"I tell you she puts sugar in the curries."

"But you like the end result, don't you?"

He would go away muttering, and like any sneak at school he became even less popular. She for her part would put him down with her withering schoolboy wit:

"*Aney*, Themis, is your third leg any better than your second? Or have you got a permanent limp there too?"

Another time he pointed out the little red spots that were beginning to appear all over the upper verandah.

"That woman doesn't stop chewing betel. And she spits it everywhere."

With her mouth full of red betel-juice I have to say Agnes was beginning to look quite a bit like a tubercular vampire. I was horrified to see more red splashes all over the green Kirman carpet in the Blue Room. I showed them to her.

"Agnes," I said, "this has got to stop."

"You're quite right," she agreed, "you'd better roll up the carpet at once."

And in my madness, I did, in my greed for all those delicious curries issuing forth from her kitchen.

The kitchen, or more accurately the cook-house, is attached to the servants' block, away from the main house. We awoke one morning to the sound of a major battle back there. When servants fight it's best not to get involved, unless you are prepared to take drastic action and sack one or other of the parties. We kept to our room. Suddenly it all went quiet. Themis came up the stairs. He looked old and weary.

"What happened?" I asked, but he just shook his head. It took awhile to coax it out of him. She had finally trounced him in their fight by dropping her cloth and exposing her bearded self: the ultimate line-room insult. He was shaking as he described it all in pungently graphic detail.

After that he retired to the banana patch behind the servants quarters to lick his wounds, and Agnes was seen doing a victory lap up and down the kitchen passage. After each battle her cooking improved accordingly: pork pickle, and stuffed crab, beef smore and black-curried shark. It was a wonder she ever got the seasoning right because she never tasted any of these dishes.

It was about this time that my friend Richard called from London.

"I'm thinking of coming out to visit for a fortnight at Easter."

Richard is one of those rich carefree bachelors, who thinks nothing of going to Rio for the Carnival or Antarctica to walk with the penguins, all at a moment's notice.

"You're in for a treat if you come," I said. "We have a loony in the house looking after the baby, but her cooking is unbelievably good."

We were all lined up on the verandah to greet him when he arrived, Devi and I with Themis on one side, and on the other, Agnes and her teeth. Richard, smooth bachelor that he is, did only the mildest of double-takes when he saw her.

Afterwards I caught him secretly taking pictures of her, with Agnes posing away like the Playmate of the Month. I found out later that he had pasted a photo of her face on the Christmas card he sent to his best enemy, his sister-in-law Delia, with the words, 'Cheer up Delia, it could be worse.'

Agnes was very happy cooking for a *suddha,* a white man, and her cooking turned positively Michelin. (Murunga flowers in scrambled egg, duck pot-roasted in arrack) The baby must have been thoroughly neglected. Did I care?

One morning Richard and I were coming out of his room past the little upstairs kitchen when he turned to me and whispered,

"Don't look now, Agnes is on the kitchen cupboards."

"At the cupboards," I corrected.

"No, she's actually standing on top of the work surface, *on* the cupboards."

I carried on walking.

"Aren't you going to say anything?"

"In this house," I replied haughtily, "we pursue the American policy on gays in the military: Don't ask, don't tell."

He was silent for a while. Then he said:

"Are you sure you want to entrust the welfare of your only child to a woman who is," he hesitated in his choice of words, "not completely of sound mind?"

"Nobody stuffs a crab better," I pointed out. And he was forced to agree.

* * *

The next week Avril, Devi's double-nannied friend, decided to throw a party for Richard: in Colombo, any excuse. Avril lives not far, in a house about a tenth the size of this, into which she has managed to insinuate a pond, a jacuzzi, a waterfall and a white marble atrium three floors high. Did I mention the tree? In the middle of the atrium there's this dirty great plastic tree which rises three floors up to the skylight in the roof. Actually, I'm just jealous. It doesn't look half as bad as I'm trying to make out. In fact it looks quite stunning.

In the interests of hygiene - little red spots all over the white marble - we arrived minus Agnes. All Devi's friends were there dressed in black, the colour of choice that year for young nannied couples. The nannies themselves were out in the garden, drinking orangeade decorously under the avocado tree.

Avril just to be bloody minded was in beige, Gucci or Pucci or whatever.

"What, no Agnes?" she asked in mock dismay. Shaking our heads we passed on. I set to work on the little bits of smoked salmon and caviar, a welcome change from the patties and cutlets I am more used to. (I only ever go anywhere for the food.) Avril bless her heart had done us proud.

I had just finished the last of the smoked oysters when she came up to me with a (matching) beige cordless phone.

"Someone called Themis for you," she said. Now we usually give Themis a contact number when we go out but never in living memory has he used it, being petrified of the phone.

"You'd better come home quick," he said.

"Why, what's happened?"

"You'd better come," he repeated and hung up. Regretfully leaving the hot prawn kebabs that were just beginning to circulate we headed back.

Agnes sat in the upper verandah, a small island in a sea of broken furniture.

"It was the man in the Upali coat," she explained. Upali's, the chocolate people, had recently been running an ad featuring a man in a *mudliyar* coat, a black coat with gold froggings that native officials used to wear in colonial times. He had enormous moustaches and a tortoiseshell comb stuck in his hair in the nineteenth century manner, and was meant to be a figure of jollity, but I could see how he might appear rather menacing to the untutored line-room eye.

"I saw his shadow in the garden," she said, "and then *patas!* he jumped right over the house." The house is forty feet high.

"Now Agnes," I said, "calm down and don't worry. You've obviously imagined it all."

"I can see *you're* the one who's worried," she replied, "but don't be. I fixed him good and proper." She pointed to the broken furniture, the mahogany sabre-legs heaped up in the middle of the verandah like the remains of some giant's fish supper.

"I had to scare him off, you see, by making a big noise. Anyway you don't mind, do you, it's only this old junk after all."

Devi and I retired to consult. Our life was just returning to normal and we were actually getting eight hours uninterrupted sleep for the first time since the baby was born. Compared to that, what was a little madness now and then?

We came back out. "Agnes, Madam and I have decided to keep you on, to give you one more chance. However, please try to be more careful in future..."

"But you don't understand!" she interrupted. "I couldn't *possibly* stay here after this. It's just not safe." She looked at us, dead serious. "I mean I know you're going through hard times, you poor things, having to eat squid and crab and all that, and I know you're tied to this broken down old house which nobody else wants, but I at least can escape. I'm *free!*"

She must have seen the shocked look on our faces.

"Don't worry," she consoled, "I gave him such a scare, he won't be back for a long while yet, I am sure."

Richard spent the rest of his holidays eating tinned food and Themis's water curries. Devi went back to her nappies and the baby to his scales. (C sharp minor.)

And me?

I'm a walking wreck, a zombie. The only small satisfaction I got was when Avril asked "Where's Agnes?" I was able to reply in the immortal words of Saki:

"She was a good cook as cooks go, and as cooks go she went."

So Agnes, if you are out there somewhere, reading this or having it read to you in your cosy line-room, please, *please,* come back. All is forgiven.

The Only Shortcoming

Mrs. Badugoda had a certain flair for the dramatic. "No doubt you all know why you are here today," she said looking round at those assembled. Of course nobody knew. And nobody knew that fact better than Mrs. B. But it was the way she liked things done.

"Rani," she said. Her husband looked at her in amazement. "Rani?" he countered mildly.

"Yes, Rani. You know, your *daughter*," she added in case her husband needed further elucidation. "For heaven's sake wake up, George."

Mrs. B. did not suffer fools gladly. She suffered her husband not at all. But she could not complain: after all, he had provided her with a gracious house and all that went with it. If you were unkind you would have said that it was in an up-and-coming area of Colombo. But once inside those gates you felt you had definitely arrived: there were tennis courts, a swimming pool, and hot and cold running servants. Then again if you were a member of the old guard you would have muttered darkly that Mrs. B was not quite *quite*, but she herself was the first to admit how proud she was of her humble origins. "It's not what you are in life, but what you make of it," she was fond of saying. And you had to admit she had made plenty of hers.

In fact there was Only One Shortcoming which marred this idyllic existence. And that was Rani.

"As you know," Mrs. B. was saying, "It's about time my daughter got married. She is quite old enough. In fact, almost too old. One more year and she will begin to get difficult." She knew, because she had been a notoriously difficult case in her day.

"I intend to set about this task," she continued, "with the help of you my closest friends." There were four of them, a Bishop, two Cabinet Ministers and my mother. My mother was the only woman there, and that, because she was safe, being just the right age. If she had been any older, she might have thrown a spanner in the works for the sheer hell of it - the women of Colombo were good with spanners - and if she had been any younger she might have been tempted to take Rani's place.

"Have you anybody in mind, Mrs. B?" the Bishop asked in his most ponderous confessional manner. Mrs. B. restrained with difficulty the urge to tell him not to be a silly old fool because she would hardly have called him here otherwise. Instead she glittered graciously and proceeded with her narrative.

"There is only one young man in this town fit to marry my daughter." All faces looked up expectantly.

"Quentin." The name fell like a skeleton in a tomb. The Cabinet Ministers sat up as if they had suddenly received a three line whip across their backsides. And the Bishop clutched the crucifix at his breast.

"You don't mean..."

"Yes I do." Mrs. B. wanted to dispel any doubt. Quentin was Colombo's most eligible bachelor, being the only son of a family that owned vast rubber estates and all the industry that went with them. He had been the best catch of the season for quite a few seasons now.

"I have broached the subject with Quentin's mother," Mrs. B was saying, "and though she is not too...Well, let us say she is not violently opposed to the idea. With her approval, I have decided to give a dinner..."

The most conscientious objector to all this was Quentin himself. It was not that he minded Rani in particular. He was, quite simply, a misogynist set in his die-hard bachelor ways and unwilling to change. He had heard enough talk of suitable wives lately. He was having none of it.

At that moment the party in the study was interrupted by the click click sound so familiar to the Badugoda household. The door opened and the Only Shortcoming popped her head in.

"Hello," she said. Other young debs might have their toy dogs or their favourite sonnets to carry around with them. Rani had her castanets. She played them with a certain zest and she played them all day. Every day. For she was a great believer in practice. And if visitors to the house found this a little hard to appreciate, she merely attributed it to their outrageous lack of musicality.

"Ah Rani dear, come and meet this nice Auntie and these Uncles," Mrs. B. said. They are about to decide your fate she might have added but didn't, for she was a great believer in not spoiling her children. Having made her greetings Rani clicked her way down the corridor, for practice makes perfect, and the little party in the study began its council of war in earnest. Never had there been a finer General to guide them. The campaign was mapped out to the last detail. It was going to be a party to end all parties...

The next day the invitations went out. After much coaxing, Quentin was persuaded to come. But he would be there on one condition, he said: that Rani wasn't. Mrs. B. called another urgent council of war, and such was her power that the ministers came halfway through their cabinet meeting. The Bishop came a little later - after communion - having dispensed with God first.

"What shall we do?" asked my mother. But a good general is equal to every occasion. "If Quentin doesn't want it, Rani won't be there," Mrs. B. said quietly, "at least not in person." Everyone wondered how that could be possible, but no one dared ask.

"But in that case, who will sit next to him?" the Bishop queried timidly. He might have been asking forgiveness from God. Mrs. B. was silent for a moment, weighing the pros and cons. A good General has to be lightning quick and his decisions have to be brilliant. She turned to my mother. "You will," she said briefly.

In the next few days the house was cleaned from top to bottom. The newly polished mirrors shone like pools and the newly-filled pool shone like, well, a mirror. On the morning of the party the dance floor arrived. Mrs. B. had ordered one specially for the occasion and the workmen set it up by the swimming pool. At tea-time the band made its appearance. Mrs. B. had fleetingly considered a castanet performance halfway through the evening, but had dropped the idea as being unsound. You could have too much of a good thing. Instead there would be some light music. Some jazz, a rhumba or two and the odd cha-cha. Quentin was not into the twist, thank God!

The kitchens were a flurry of activity. When the first guests began to arrive, Rani could be seen drifting in and out of the dining room in a floaty chiffon number. What she thought about all this was really anybody's guess but there was an *other-worldly* look on her face which stopped anyone from asking. Was she the lamb being led to the slaughter? Was she the spider being hospitable to the fly? She probably didn't know herself.

Mrs. B. glittered regally at the top of the staircase in lace and black pearls. Quentin's parents arrived, with a reluctant Quentin in tow. He was introduced to my mother and when dinner was announced he accompanied her in. He was not a great conversationalist at the best of times, our Quentin, but that day he seemed even more sombre than usual. Something was weighing heavily on his mind. My mother did her best. She chattered away brightly about this that and the other. Quentin remained silent about this and that, his mind dwelling probably on the other.

Rani was nowhere to be seen. But the food was superb. Course followed course and as the evening wore on Quentin's mood mellowed. He actually began to laugh at the jokes being told around the table. He even supplied a few himself. Mrs. B who sat far away at the head, majestically aloof and ruthlessly charming, missed nothing. This was her finest hour. The evening was going to be a resounding success and the cat was, so to speak, in the bag. She raised her wineglass in a silent toast, and the Bishop hastily made a sign of the cross.

Suddenly there was a hush. Two servants in white coats pattered in bearing the pièce de résistance, followed rather coyly by Rani.

"The Crinoline Lady," announced Mrs. B. as the pudding was placed on the table amid the oohs and aahs of the dinner-guests. "It was made by my daughter." Rani was reluctant to accept credit for something the cook had taken days to prepare but everyone loves a reticent genius and the guests became even more appreciative. Even Quentin admitted that the pudding was superb. The fact that Rani had made it was neither here nor there, but he was too polite to say so.

Soon afterwards the party came to an end. As the guests drifted away in twos and threes, Mrs. B. bade goodbye to Quentin and his family. She retired to bed exhausted by victory and slept the sleep of a four-star general…

"Well wasn't that a *lovely* party!" exclaimed Quentin's mother on the way home. The driver understood English, so the real post-mortem would have to wait till they were back at the house, but Quentin's mother was impatient. She wanted to probe her son's mind, like the *vedah* who gently probes his patient's stomach to divine some hidden, inner malady.

Quentin stared fixedly into the middle distance, or more accurately into the back of the driver's neck.

"All those lovely lights, and that band," his mother was saying.

"The Rubber Band," murmured Quentin.

"What was that?" his mother asked sharply, but Quentin merely giggled. There was a glazed look about his eyes and his spectacles flashed sinisterly in the dark. Driver or no driver Quentin's mother decided to come right out with it.

"Well Quentin, wasn't there anyone there, any particular girl who caught your fancy?" She closed her eyes as visions of her future daughter-in-law swam into view, to the sound of wild castanets.

"Yes," Quentin nodded, pushing his glasses back up his nose. Quentin's mother held her breath.

"I rather liked the girl sitting next to me," said Quentin feebly.

The Knights of Saint Gregory

The last person I expected to see at Gatwick Airport was Uncle Sid.

"I've come to take you home for the weekend."

"Uncle Sid," I said getting annoyed, "you're not taking me anywhere. School is only one stop away from here. I'm completely jet-lagged as it is and I need the sleep. Term starts Monday morning."

"But today is Saturday," he protested.

"I've got my mocks this term. I need to study."

"Come on, come on, don't be so wet!"

But I said nothing.

"They're all waiting for you."

I continued looking ahead, silent. I thought to myself, it's amazing how green England looks, even after just four weeks away.

"Auntie Charm has cooked your favourite devilled pork." He looked at me sideways to see if I was mellowing. "You know how you *love* her devilled pork." I began to smile. It's always like this with Uncle Sid. You can't remain angry with him for long, he's such a lovable old crook. So we got into his car and drove off towards London, the opposite direction to school. And just as I was relenting and beginning to have good thoughts about him, he pulled over into a petrol station. He filled up for four pounds fifty, a lot of petrol in those days. Then he looked at me and waited. I tried ignoring him but after a while it got to me. I got out of the car and went over and paid. My father had just given me five pounds pocket money to last the term: I now had exactly fifty pence left.

Sid was vaguely related to my Father. Every *abroad boy* at school had to have a guardian and Sid was mine, though the school would have had hysterics if they knew what he was really like. He had been named Siddartha by his parents in an excess of zeal, but as soon as he arrived in England he became Sid, and this was much more to his taste: it suited his colourful wide-boy image, larger than life and twice as handsome. After all, you spend your whole life trying to live up to the name your parents so thoughtlessly give you, and perhaps the real misfits in life are the ones who can't. Siddartha would have been too much for him I think.

"Welcome to Diamondwood Rise," he said, as we drove up to his latest house. Sid's father was a big cheese back home. Amongst other things, he was a Knight of St.Gregory, and you never knew whether Sid was proud of that fact or ashamed.

"I've spent my whole life avoiding them," he said. "Maybe they'll never find me here in jolly suburbia." I had visions of a band of old men in faded green velvet riding through the forests of New Malden.

The house may have been small but there were plenty of people inside. I ignored them all and went into the kitchen where Aunty Charm was frying tomatoes. She was small and birdlike with masses of frizzy hair and glasses that pointed upwards at the corners.

"So you're back?"

I nodded.

"You look exhausted. Go and get some sleep. I'll wake you when lunch is ready."

Uncle Sid took my suitcase up, managing the narrow staircase easily for a man so large, with a strange gangling sort of elegance. He put my suitcase down in the small room over the front door, my usual room.

"I've left you a present," he said.

There was a freshly-minted copy of Playboy on the bed.

"Uncle Sid!" I said horrified, "you know I don't read that sort of thing!"

"Oh sure," he replied and shut the door.

About once a month in term-time I took the train up from Three Bridges, negotiating the subterranean tunnels of

Clapham Junction to wherever Uncle Sid happened to be at the time. When I first knew him, he lived in a cavernous old house in Warwick Avenue. "Every other house contains a Maharajah," he said proudly, "I'm just about the only commoner here." But too much good living, or a lack of money, or perhaps even the Knights of St.Gregory had driven him onwards and downwards, to Dollis Hill, then Cricklewood and finally here.

Sid had had a perfectly decent life back home in Sri Lanka, which included amongst other things a perfectly decent wife. He was always fond of the good life. Once, at one of his innumerable parties, he found fault with the chicken curry because there were too many bones in it. A tremendous row ensued in front of scandalised party guests, the poor wife got it in the neck, and things went beyond the point of no return. There was a parting of the ways. Divorce was out of the question for a good Catholic boy like Sid: I don't know how he managed but he got the marriage annulled (wicked people even said the Knights of St. Gregory had a hand). It was probably the first time in the history of Christendom that a marriage was dissolved for the sake of a chicken bone. Leaving behind an excess of ex in-laws baying for blood Sid escaped to London where he married the first girl that came along, his landlady's daughter Auntie Chamari.

After a couple of hours sleep that day, I came down to find that the party had matured. There was a golden tinge round the party guests rather like the saints in those holy pictures they give you at school. There was a man up a ladder painting the outside of the house. He had a bottle of beer in one hand and a paintbrush in the other. Every once in a while he tried to sneak inside to watch the Test match going on, on the telly, and Uncle Sid vigorously chased him back out. I had never before seen a Sri Lankan workman in England. I was appalled and fascinated. There were the usual girls from the High Commission and men in suits and a concert pianist whom I loathed because he always tried to bully me into playing even though I was really, really bad. Maybe because it made *his* playing sound really, really good. In the middle of all this, Auntie Charm went about her daily business, cooking and cleaning, refilling the guests glasses and cleaning out the ashtrays. But I was not allowed to relax.

"Ashok," said Uncle Sid, "the garden, please."

Every month this happened and every month I felt outraged. I did not come to England to weed other people's flower-beds, I thought bitterly. I settled in at the farther end of the garden with revenge on my mind. When in doubt, pull it out, I said to myself viciously. Strange how those suburban English flowers continued to flourish in spite of my violent attentions every month.

I had just about finished the weeding when I felt rather than heard a slight commotion at the door, a sussurrus of silk. Miss Saravanamoottoo had arrived, all glossy and honey-coloured and wrapped in six yards of the finest. I never quite knew who she was or what she did for a living, only that she always turned up at some point of the proceedings and when she did, things became hot! hot! hot!

The men in suits undid their collars.

"Don't come anywhere near me,"

Miss Saravanamoottoo warned loudly, so they immediately got closer, "I stink! Last night I covered my entire body from head to toe in *gingelly* oil and slept on newspapers."

The image of this was almost too much to bear.

"I only do this when I sleep alone, of course…" A low musical laugh.

"…and when I woke up this morning I was *covered* in newsprint."

"What's black and gold and read all over?" asked one of the suits joyously.

"Miss Saravanamoottoo!" shouted another.

It may have been getting hot in the sitting room but back there in the kitchen the temperature dropped a degree or so. I was the only one to notice. Auntie Charm calmly went about chopping garlic or grinding chillies or whatever else she was doing, not bothering much about entertaining the guests, and I was backstage with her. She and I had the bit parts in the play, and that was enough for us.

Towards the end of the day, as usual, there was a fight. That afternoon was one of the worst. Uncle Sid wanted to drop Miss Saravanamoottoo home. The guests had mostly gone but she lingered on in the garden, shimmering like a haze in the middle distance, a sort of suburban *houri* among the mangled roses.

"What about me?" Auntie Charm was shouting from the top of the stairs. "All I do is cook and clean and scrub!" She was brushing the stair-carpet vigorously with a dustpan brush.

"It's only up to Putney," Uncle Sid said apologetically. "I won't be long."

"You're still like the lodger you were in my mother's house," Auntie Charm continued, "come and go as you please. Everything done for you. Except now you don't have to pay. You have it all for free!" She gave a small bitter laugh.

"I always did," he said softly but she did not hear, she was too busy with her brushing.

"I'm just the bitch on the stairs!" she screamed, "only here for the housework, not good enough for all your posh friends!"

Then she saw me standing at the bottom of the stairs and straightened up. "Take the boy with you," she said. "He'll make sure you don't get up to anything."

And so I went with them in the back of the car to Putney, where Miss Saravanamoottoo lived, in a purpose-built gray block of flats quite unsuited to her exotic temperament.

"Shan't be long," she said as they got out of the car. She put a finger on my nose and pressed gently.

"You be a good boy now."

They were gone nineteen minutes. I timed them by my brand new silver-coloured Timex watch. It didn't seem long to a child of thirteen. But I know now that nineteen minutes is a long time in anyone's life, long enough to change the course of their fate.

I never saw Miss Saravanamoottoo again. As time went on and I got older, my visits to Uncle Sid got less and less frequent, till finally I lost touch entirely. I heard that they had brought over a maid from Sri Lanka to help Auntie Charm with the housework. How they got her the visa I don't know. Maybe the Knights of St.Gregory. And then, predictably, Uncle Sid left Auntie Charm and returned to Sri Lanka with the maid, setting up house with her in a suburb of Colombo. His sisters said to my father: "How can we *possibly* have them back in the house again? *She* will come too, and then she'll have to use the back door and leave her shoes outside."

✛ ✛ ✛

Yesterday, I went to his funeral. The place was crawling with ex-wives but I ran Auntie Charm to earth in the kitchen, keeping her head well down. She was still exactly as I remembered. She looked at me through her pointy glasses, like a sort of intelligent, recently-widowed bird.

"So I see they got him in the end," I said.

"Who?" she asked suspiciously.

"The Knights of St.Gregory," I said. But she had forgotten that old joke. I am not even sure she recognised me, all grizzled and paunchy as I am now.

Anyway, I put my arms round her and hugged her. I hugged her in gratitude for her very superior devilled pork; and for being just about the only one back then to treat me the way I should have been treated, as a child. But mostly I guess I hugged her in sorrow, for the unspoken complicity of those nineteen minutes, long lost but never entirely forgotten.

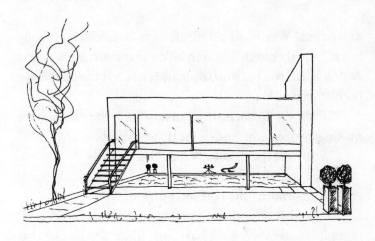

Colpetty People

My best friend Niloo called from Colombo.

"You'd better get here quick," she said, "half of Colombo is after him, mothers, daughters, grand mothers . . ."

"Ok, ok I get the picture," I said. I had already read the news in the Silver Bullet, the Sri Lankan expat paper in London. Gnanam had been knocked down and killed by a train while walking on the tracks, and Ayoub was devastated. Was it an accident? Was it suicide? Nobody knew, nobody cared. The only thing that mattered was that Ayoub Khan was back on the market again at the tender age of forty-eight.

"Even the women who came to cook the dhana were making eyes at him. And as for that garden boy. . ."

"Spare me the details, Niloo," I said curtly.

"Tell me when your flight is, and I'll get him to meet you at the airport," she said and hung up.

She didn't offer to send me the money, of course, even though she knows I don't have any. Little details like that somehow manage to escape Niloo, now that she's married to that film producer of hers who is positively oozing with the stuff.

So I rang up my son in Leeds.

"Haresh I need to fly to Sri Lanka, and I need to ask you a big favour."

"No Ma, I have no money. This is England, remember? I have a mortgage on the house and payments on my car and I still haven't finished paying for last year's holiday."

"Haresh," I began, and maybe I was sounding a little desperate, "Gnanam has been killed, I have to get home." Just then the doorbell rang. "Hang on a sec," I said, "till I get the door."

"No, Ma," he replied sweetly, "you call me back. And remember, no loans."

Children! You hang on nine long months for them. They can't be bothered to wait two seconds for you.

It was Loelia at the door, my next-door neighbour. Rich, Colombian, wears her emeralds to Sainsburys, you know the type. Actually she comes to *me* when she runs short of anything, Sainsburys being only her second destination of choice.

"I've come to borrow some sugar," she says.

"Lo, I need to borrow six hundred pounds," I say. You have to be direct with these South Americans, grab them by their metaphorical balls, so to speak.

"Sure, *querida*, but I'll be wanting interest."

So I give her a pound of sugar.

৯ ৯ ৯

Ayoub met me at the airport, looking every bit as gorgeous as the day he walked down the aisle with my best friend Gnanam. Even then he used to look at me in a funny way so I knew there was something there, but you don't poach on your best friend's territory, do you? Actually, there were three of us back then, Niloo, Gnanam and I. The Three Muses, I used to call us, because I was the literary one. Gnanam was the clever dreamy one who went on to become a research chemist, much in demand for her work on drugs-dumping in Third World countries. She ended up marrying her childhood sweetheart amidst much family disapproval. Niloo on the other hand always had her eye to the main chance, and she found her film producer soon enough. I was the chain-smoking foul-mouthed one who scared men off, and, I tell you, these Sri Lankan men scare easily. But people used to tell me I was some looker then, though I've let myself run to seed now. It isn't easy to look *svelte* when you're living on baked beans and chips every day.

So I took myself off to England and found Barry - lazy, good-looking Barry - big on ideas, small on brains. Bungalow Barry, they used to call him, because he had nothing upstairs but plenty below. When my father died I brought out the money he left me from the sale of the family house in Colpetty, and do you know, I have *no* idea where it all went? Of course there was Haresh by then, and children can be expensive little beasts, but mostly it went on Barry. To cut a long and dismal story short, when the money ran out, so did Barry, and I found myself in this council flat in Putney, fucked and far from home. Not that we don't have our moments, Loelia and I. I always say that in London you can be poor in quite a *decent* way, though Loelia is not poor; only pretends to be, for my benefit and the taxman's.

૭ ૭ ૭

"Padma!" Ayoub said, when I arrived at the airport, "you haven't changed one little bit!"

"Oh coupez le crap!" I replied, "And get this bag into the car. And while you're at it put my suitcase in as well."

Oh but how Colombo has changed since I was last here! It never gets better: only noisier and busier and dirtier: just more and more of the same old smelly old thing.

Ayoub told me how much he had always loved me, even from those days. Of course he had loved Gnanam too.

"It's not that you loved me less," I elaborated, "but you loved her more."

"What do you mean?" he turned to me aggressively.

"Oh nothing. Just a joke." I wasn't up to explaining literary allusions after fifteen hours on a plane.

When we got into town he said, "Now Padma, I think we have to be grown up about this thing. We're both middle-aged people after all, and consenting adults. You can come home with me."

"*You* can consent all you want," I replied somewhat tartly. "I'm off to the *Renuka*, so drive me there like a good boy please."

The *Renuka* is a quiet, comfortable, unpretentious hotel in Colpetty. My father used to tell me when I was small, "Remember, Padma, that we're *Colpetty people*." I truly believed then, that there was something special about those of us fortunate enough to live there. But Colpetty itself is bisected down the middle by the Galle Road, the main road south, which follows the coast at some distance inland. Everything between the Galle Road and the sea is called Colpetty Seaside, the rest being the Landside. We lived on the landside, where people were serious and fine and upstanding, and infinitely dull. But when you crossed that imaginary line down the middle of Galle road to the other side, the magic began: the air became clear and light, the atmosphere lifted. Maybe because you were close to the sea, but, for whatever reason, there was a carnival atmosphere about that side which was faintly raffish. There were diamond points of light in people's eyes, they laughed louder, they enjoyed themselves more. Seaside people seemed to spend their whole life going from christening to wedding to dhana, and work was the last thing on their minds.

Ayoub lived on the Seaside, and my father never quite approved.

"You'll see, he'll never amount to much," he used to warn me.

"He doesn't need to," I would reply. "That land he's sitting on is worth an absolute fortune." And it was true. The Americans, the Brits and the Indians were all building their embassies on that side of the Galle road, and seaside land was beginning to fetch unbelievable prices. Ayoub truly didn't care. He never behaved in that insufferably pretentious manner that rich people sometimes have, and he continued going round in his sarong and chappals, always smiling, always carefree.

"If we're going to do this, let's do it properly," he said to me as he dropped me off at the hotel.

And he did. He proposed to me the next day and married me a week later.

I wore a brown and blue sari (the bride wore brown!) Actually it was rather beautiful, even though I chose it in about five minutes flat. I've always had an eye for colour.

Niloo, bless her heart, threw a wedding reception for us at the Taj, all starlets and harlots and aged impresarios with blue-black hair. I was told about fifteen times what a *super* couple Ayoub and Gnanam had been and how well she had looked after him and how lucky he was to have been married to her. Of course nobody remembered, as I did, the furore that the wedding caused back then because they were from two different communities with two different religions. And nobody thought to mention their son Akbar who had come over from New Zealand for his mother's funeral, but couldn't be bothered or didn't have time, to come back for his father's second marriage.

I wanted to shout to my wedding guests: "You don't know the first thing about Ayoub and Gnanam! *I* was their friend, not you, and I knew how they really were, and they were neither better nor worse than you and me." But I held my peace. The new bride must at all times smile and show her teeth and behave like the worthy Colpetty person that she is. Instead I began to speculate idly how many of these harlots and starlets were wishing they were in my shoes.

When we got back home that night Ayoub said, "Now Padma, I know you might be expecting me to carry you across the threshold."

"I know all about your hernia," I replied. "You're forgiven."

I always think it faintly disgusting when a Colpetty person over forty five begins discussing their sex life, so you'll just have to be satisfied when I tell you it was worth the twenty year wait.

৩ ৩ ৩

Ayoub Khan's house was built in the 1950's, large and ugly and *moderne*, with a sweeping circular staircase and mosaics of many-coloured marbles, all in the best Terry Jonklass manner. It would have looked good in Manhattan. I could imagine the starlets and harlots tripping lightly down the staircase like a litterful of kittens. Alas it was wasted on me. All I could see was the dust, the dust, the dust!

I may be poor in England but Loelia will tell you I run a tight ship. You can eat off my floors.

I don't want to get all preachy on you right here, but what's with you Sri Lankans, with your wet, cockroach infested bathrooms and your unspeakable kitchens? Not that I was blaming Ayoub: he had to cope with the death of his wife and housekeeping would have been the last thing on his mind. I came down next morning all fired up to cook Ayoub his breakfast. I took one look at the kitchen and came right back out. Ayoub found me in a state of shock.

"Have you seen the kitchen?" I asked. He didn't seem to know what I was on about.

"Oh, leave all that to Wimla, that's her province," he replied, Wimla being the daily.

"But don't you ever feel like going in there to fix yourself a cup of tea?"

He looked surprised.

And there were more surprises in store for me. At the bottom of the stairs there was a small indoor garden with a concrete pergola overhead. A pathway of granite crazy paving led to a room with a reeded glass door that was kept locked.

"Ayoub, what goes on in there?" I asked.

"That? Oh that's Gnanam's lab where she does her research," he replied.

"*Was* Gnanam's lab, you mean?"

"Yes, but I'd prefer it if you kept it that way. It's got all her things in it. I haven't been in there since she, since she..." He was beginning to look upset, so I dropped the subject.

"Anyway what are our plans for today?" I asked.

"We have Zulfikar's mother's *kaththam*. And don't make any plans for tomorrow because Gayathri has attained age, so they're expecting us round." *Ghastly* thought.

I don't think it had occurred to Ayoub that even though we hadn't gone anywhere for our honeymoon, I might want him all to myself for even just a little while. That evening, after an exhausting *kaththam* and a long and luxurious nap - Putney seemed so far away! - Ayoub said:

"I'm off to the gym now."

"Aren't you a bit old to be going to gyms?" Cruel of me I know.

"You know I never miss it. It's like a religion to me."

"Shall I come?"

"Well…" he hesitated. "I'm not sure I like the thought of all those men ogling you. Anyway there are very few women there. One or two young girls."

What he meant was, it was all right for him to go at his age, but not for me at mine.

"I'm going for a walk," I said haughtily, "I don't know what time I'll be back."

And I went for my walk down the Galle Road: past the bookshops and the casinos, past Sri Lankan skyscrapers of three and four stories that seemed to look derelict no sooner were they built, past the windows of McDonalds where women in diamonds stared hungrily at passers-by. It was dark when I got back but Ayoub was not home. I felt like a stranger returning to what was still Gnanam's house, and a small, disloyal thought floated into my mind of my warm clean flat in Putney.

ఌ   ఌ   ఌ

As the days went by I made a mental list of the things that had to change. The kitchen had to be redone, the bathroom suite definitely had to go, and why oh why were we still sleeping on Gnanam's bed? I discovered that in Sri Lanka you may be rich as Croesus, but you think nothing of using the same things year in year out till they positively disintegrate on you. Was I being unfair expecting hot water on tap and new sheets on the bed? What bugged me most of all, actually, was the lab that was kept permanently locked.

"I had a dream," Ayoub said. "I saw Gnanam far away across the railway tracks. She was in a red sari and she was beckoning to me. And I couldn't help myself, I began walking towards her. Just then a train thundered past, missing me by inches. The shock of the noise and the wind rushing by brought me to my senses and I woke up. And the funny thing, you know, I could actually hear a train in the distance."

I stubbed out my cigarette in the remains of Wimla's breakfast egg.

"Ghost stories," I said.

ఌ   ఌ   ఌ

It felt strange, this life of leisure. In London I had this part-time job with the council's housing department. By the time I finished work, did the shopping, and got home, cooked dinner and cleaned up, it was time for bed. What little shopping there was to do over here was done by Wimla. I barely went into the kitchen because I did not have to, and - strange to say - I found after a few days I couldn't even rouse up enough enthusiasm or energy to attack the dust. It was almost as if I was beginning to see it all through Ayoub's eyes, which meant not seeing it at all.

We were hardly there: every day there was some function to attend and we only came home to sleep.

The hours that hung heaviest were the hours that Ayoub was away at the gym, in the early evening. I took to walking along the tracks, by the edge of the sea. The sunsets were spectacular I suppose, but all I could see was the litter strewn around the rails, the boulders piled high against erosion, the syringes and the condoms. It was not the beach I had known in my youth. There were groups of young men loitering in the twilight. One of them said when I passed, "Machang did you see that tourist *baduwa*?" and I have to say I was pleased no end. I never saw anyone in a red sari beckoning to me seductively across the tracks.

ॐ   ॐ   ॐ

Then one day I came down to find the reeded-glass door open and Wimla inside, whistling to herself. By the way, I don't think I have introduced Wimla to you properly and it is high time I did so. Wimla is a mountain of a woman with very sparse hair done up in a top-knot, who comes to work every morning in a loud checked sarong and a very *very* dirty white blouse. She reminds me of the 'before' woman in the *Sunlight* soap ad, and there are days when I long to rip the blouse off her back and wash it with my own fair hands, but I don't because she would only get the wrong idea. I can't imagine she's the one who made eyes at Ayoub Khan over the dhana dishes but then again this is Sri Lanka.

"Who told you to open this room?" I asked her sternly, but she looked at me boldly and continued whistling. Ayoub was away in courts on one of his numerous land cases. He must have left her the key. The room was full, with boxes and boxes of pills, samples I suppose of various drugs imported into the country. There were a couple of metal lab stools and a long wooden table on which were the tools of Gnanam's trade: the burettes and pipettes, the Bunsen burners and crucibles filled with coloured crystals. There were calipers and sharp cutting instruments and a red wicked looking electric drill. Gnanam's blue lab coat hung on a hook behind the door. Strangely, there was not a speck of dust anywhere, only an all-pervasive smell of pharmaceuticals.

Ayoub came back from court at lunchtime but I never had the courage to ask him what had made him change his mind about the room. His income, what little there was of it, depended on the rentals from his various properties. A lot of these were occupied by sitting tenants from whom it was difficult to extract rent, though this did not seem to stop them enjoying lifestyles much higher than his own. There was this particular woman he told me about who had once made a huge fuss about paying. A week later his friend met her on the London flight flying first class, with the children and ayah in economy. This was particularly galling to Ayoub who had never flown first class in his life.

Although Ayoub Khan was very rich on paper, he was, I guess, quite poor in actual fact. The kitchen, the bathroom, the hot water all remained undone owing to lack of funds. I used to wonder in my more idle moments - and there were many of those - how the harlots and starlets would have coped. Don't get me wrong here, it's not that I'm complaining, but the lack of cash never seemed to stop him giving the most lavish presents wherever we went.

"Us Colpetty people have certain standards to maintain," he would say.

Meanwhile I continued having cold baths with my Colpetty cockroaches.

∾   ∾   ∾

Next day the rains broke. The Seaside was cut up and lit by the vicious colours of the monsoon, purple and acid yellow and bone grey. By opening the reeded glass door we seemed to have unleashed other forces too.

"Do you think I'm ill?" I asked Wimla when she brought my afternoon tea. On the saucer by the side of the cup was a test tube. Hastily she took it away and brought me a spoon.

That night I went up to bed a few moments before
Ayoub. On my night table was a bottle of pills and a glass of
water. There were bubbles in the water as if it had just been
poured. I could almost hear Gnanam's soothing voice
saying, "Drink up like a good girl, drink up. Swallow them
all and you can have a nice *long* rest."

The magic of the seaside was beginning to turn black.

I heard Ayoub's footsteps outside and I quickly
managed to sweep the pills into the bin before he walked in.

In the middle of all this mayhem, Niloo rang.

"Darling! You know what day it is tomorrow?" *No I
don't.*

"It's my birthday. I want you both to come for pot-
luck. I've asked very few people, only my *closest* friends." *All
sixty-eight of them.*

∾ ∾ ∾

We set off in the middle of a storm, Ayoub in shirt and
tie, me in my one good sari, the brown and blue. The rain
slashed at us like knives. Niloo's house was in the wilds of
Kotte. It wasn't in the wilds, Ayoub assured me, but it felt
like it. We went up hill, down dale and through the bush,
skirting large tracts of water where the road had gone under.
Stray cows on the verges zoomed in and out of focus and a
lone woman under a petromax lamp brandished a *pathola
karala* at us in a threatening manner as we shot past.

Niloo had been acting quite funny lately. Having
married me off, so to speak, she had dumped me. Not a
word, not a phone call, nothing. I tried calling. On the rare

occasion she came to the phone she apologised profusely: she had a rigorous beauty regime throughout the day, she said, which left her little time for idle chit-chat. It wasn't the old Niloo I knew. The new Niloo moved in a tinselled, glittery world that functioned only at night, where men dyed their hair and wore medallions and women stopped growing at thirty-nine. She genuinely loved it and it was what she had always wanted, so who could blame her? I often wondered how she regarded me: as the Little Old Maid of Putney, no doubt, enduring the rigours of a Colpetty seaside.

Well, this little old maid was under siege, and there was nobody she could turn to, not even her best friend.

Niloo's house was a long low concrete affair, entirely glassed in and brilliantly lit like some sort of glamorous fish tank. As Ayoub was parking the car I leant over and pulled out a rubber tube from his shirt pocket.

"What's this?" I asked.

"Oh that. It's Gnanam's. It's the tube off her distilling apparatus." I tell you he looked more embarrassed than if it had been some other woman's bra. I didn't ask him what it was doing there. I left it on the seat and got out of the car.

Niloo swam out to meet us, the brightest goldfish in the bowl.

"Happy birthday darling." I kissed her on both cheeks.

She looked me up and down, scrutinising the brown and blue.

"Always the bride, I see, never the bridesmaid."

"Yes, well, I had nothing else posh enough."

"You know, dear, you must learn one thing if you're going to live in this place. You can never be seen in the same sari twice. In fact there's a school of thought which says you must never be seen in the same sari *once*. Women here have been known to go upstairs and change their kit halfway through the evening."

Giggling, we went inside.

A little later on she cornered me behind a potted croton.

"So how's it going, darling?"

"Ok, I suppose."

"I mean, is he looking after you all right?"

"Why wouldn't he? He's always had a soft spot for me, he says. Though I can't help feeling he's still a little fixated on Gnanam." I was thinking of the rubber tube.

"Actually, I fear it's the other way round," she replied, looking at me speculatively. But I didn't quite understand then what she meant.

∞ ∞ ∞

My two months of unpaid leave were coming to an end. Every day I kept meaning to call the Housing Department to say I was not coming back, and every day I put it off. Ayoub continued going to the gym, sublimely indifferent to the loneliness of those long afternoons. It was at these times that I usually found the signs: once there was a long row of Gnanam's red pill boxes arranged in my medicine cabinet. Another time her instruments were laid out in neat place-settings round the dining table, fork caliper and spoon, fork caliper and spoon.

"Why me?" I kept asking myself, "What have I done to deserve all this?"

You will wonder why I didn't go to Ayoub with my little tales of woe. I wonder too, now, when I think about it sometimes. But I know it wouldn't have helped, and there was a very important reason why.

Beneath all his lazy carefree existence, Ayoub was a devout Muslim, and his religion gave him an inner discipline that I frequently envied. He didn't believe in magic, and would have been horrified that under his very own roof there was someone who even dared entertain its possibility. Magic did not exist for him therefore he was immune to it. I, who had lived abroad for much of my life and had no religion, had no resistance at all: I had succumbed to it completely. Ayoub I simply could not turn to. At the very least he would think I was making it all up and I could not bear that.

Instead, I tried getting angry with Wimla, but she ignored me: she probably had a good laugh behind my back with the other servant-women of the seaside. I was reminded of Princess Diana's famous phrase: there are three of us in this marriage. Finally, in desperation, I forced myself to call Niloo.

I caught her in between a massage and a manicure.

"Do you have any idea what's going on here?" I asked. There was a pause. I think she was weighing her words carefully.

"I've always known," she said.

"Why didn't you tell me?" I asked desperately, "Why did you drag me all this way across the ocean and foist this marriage on me when you knew…?"

"I didn't *foist* anything on you my dear," she countered smartly. "Wasn't this what you always wanted? Even when you were young, when Ayoub and Gnanam got married, didn't you always think it should have been *you* walking down that aisle?"

I was silent.

"I knew it," she continued, "I could always see it in your eyes. So get in there, fight back, assert yourself. You're in command now, and whatever black magic there is will go away."

It was easy for her to say. I put the phone down feeling even more unhappy. I was really on my own on this one.

℘   ℘   ℘

Next day Loelia called.

"Hola, que tal?"

Relations were a little frosty between us just then: I had only called to tell her about the wedding a week after it happened, and she had been more than a little shocked.

"I called to find out how you doing."

"Fine," I said wearily, "I'm just fine."

"You don't sound it."

"Actually, Lo, I'm not fine at all. There's something I need to talk to you about." I began trying to explain, but she cut in calmly: "You're having second thoughts about him, that's all it is."

"Are you crazy? This is not about him at all! This is about what's happening to *me*. There's some evil influence here, some weird thing going on."

"How do you mean weird?"

"Lo," I whispered, "*someone or something doesn't want me to be here…*"

There was silence at the other end of the line.

"But I guess you wouldn't understand about all that…"

"What do you mean I wouldn't understand? You think you Sri Lankans have the monopoly on black magic? I'm from Colombia, remember, the heartland of voodoo. *Querida,*" she continued, "take my advice, get the hell out of there! You can't afford to mess about with things like this. No man is worth all that grief."

I got angry with her. "Are you out of your mind? For the first time in my life I have peace and comfort and stability with a man I love, and you're asking me to give up all that?" I slammed the phone down.

Peace? Comfort? Stability? Who was *I* trying to kid?

જ   જ   જ

That night Ayoub had a Rotary meeting, members only, no spouses allowed rather to my relief. I wandered around the house in the eerie white light of the long-life bulbs. If this had been Putney I reflected, I would have had a glass of wine, a long hot bath and bed. The hot bath was out and there was no wine in the house, this being Colombo where the only word they understand is whisky. I went to bed wondering whether this was quite what I had in mind by a second marriage.

It can't have been even midnight when I woke up with a start. Ayoub wasn't back, but I could hear noises downstairs. I went to the stairwell and called out, "Ayoub?"

There was no answer. I could hear the scrape of a metal lab stool against the floor and the thirsty hiss of a Bunsen burner. Somebody was scraping out a crucible.

"Ayoub!" I shouted wildly.

No answer. I could hear the low moan of the drill being tried out.

They're getting ready to experiment on me, I thought.

I went to the cupboard and pulled out my small suitcase. I was out of the bedroom in five minutes flat. I ran down the staircase. There was a flickering blue light behind the reeded glass door and I could see Gnanam's lab coat moving against the glass. Someone let out a weary sigh, and as I watched, the door began to open.

I screamed.

I don't know how I found myself outside, but next thing I knew I was running down the Galle Road, my breath exploding in my ears. I ran past the bookshops and casinos, past the women in diamonds staring hungrily from the windows of McDonald's. It wasn't late but the Galle Road was virtually deserted.

I picked up my suitcase and heaved it across the road: to the side I knew best, the side I should never really have left in the first place: the Landside of Colpetty.

Tuscany

The white tiles with their luminous green streaks were cunningly laid to give an impression of depth. So that you felt you were walking over the greenery of some milky pond, or over the green shoots of rice plants in a paddy-field. The bath was full. Its throaty gurgle changed to a plaintive moan. Ashoka slid gracefully into its clutches.

Ricefields. What did he know about ricefields? Villagers standing knee-deep in the mud, singing as they bent over their back-breaking task. Seen through the window of a car a long time ago, forbidden to the touch. Had he ever stood in one? How could he, when he had been locked away in a Benedictine public school all his life? Even if there were ricefields in Sussex, he thought, the monks would not stand for it. They would get their cassocks wet.

Liquid brown children playing by green-gold fields. False gods, false *foreign* gods of rice, stolen from somebody else's temple to be worshipped secretly at his own. But were they not his gods too? And his country? The cold voice of reason was useless against the other more insistent one. *You betrayed me by leaving for another land. Discarded me. My language for somebody else's. My culture. My religion. You are a traitor.*

So now he was here, midway between heart and head. Between the country which spurned him as fiercely as he longed for it and the one whose Judas-like embrace was beginning to squeeze the life out of him. He was in Italy, that narrow limb between heaven and hell, where time did not exist.

The hazy Tuscan sunlight crept through the slats of the wooden shutters and fell on the marble floor. Absolute peace. Luisa was singing in the kitchen as she prepared lunch. He closed his eyes and he was back in heaven, where the street-urchins sang as they plucked mangoes from the trees. Where the crab-man uttered his peculiar chant as he wheeled his cart, and the servants ran out to the road and brought back a sackful of crawling green monsters which the cook emptied dramatically into the kitchen sink.

A long time ago. So that all those clearly etched memories were superimposed, like the frames of a motion-picture, cut up and stuck together, layer upon layer, to form a single image. A still. So that time did not exist there either.

He would have to go back, that was certain. But there was work to be done first. He had to return to hell to pack his bags, tidy up loose ends. He couldn't leave without saying goodbye to Beelzebub and his crew at their Sussex hangout.

The bathwater muttered threateningly as he turned on his side, and for one moment he was sad because he wished he could be suspended in this fluid for eternity, motionless. But the film had to be rerun. Timelessness was an illusion, even here in Tuscany. As if to reinforce this verdict Luisa came whistling down the passage and poked her head round the door.

"Lunch is ready. Hurry up or you'll miss your train to London. There's no time."

No time? He thought drowsily. If there was no time why all the fuss?

"What are we eating?" he asked as he stepped out of the bath.

"Risotto alla Milanese."

Oh God, not rice, he thought miserably as he slopped his way to the door.

Who Wants To Be
A Millionaire?

The postman handed Frankie a letter through the window of the front room. This was unusual. He normally threw the mail over the garden wall, sublimely indifferent to the rigours of the Sri Lankan tropical seasons. You either got your letters in a pulpy mass during the monsoons or as hot parchment coloured biscuits in the dry months. But this was different, a long heavy white envelope with an English stamp, and it deserved special treatment.

The letter was from Peter Scholl and Company, Solicitors. Frankie felt as if he was on "Who wants to be a Millionaire?" when he opened it.

"Dear Mr. Bandara," it said, "We are pleased to inform you that under the terms and conditions of the Last Will and Testament of your late godmother Mrs. Muriel Perera, you are the beneficiary of a bequest of ten thousand pounds sterling ..."

"Not bad news, I hope?" asked the postman hopefully.

"On the contrary, very good," said Frankie. Disappointed, the postman went off. Frankie took the letter to Mala, who was unpacking vegetables from a straw bag in the kitchen.

"I have an idea," he said, when she had finished reading it.

"Oh go on with you, you and your damn fool ideas!" she replied. Mala was the sweetest, cuddliest wife imaginable, with sleepy eyes and a softly rounded belly, but she had inherited language from her mother's side. Ignoring her tone, Frankie continued:

"We use the ten thousand as a deposit, get a mortgage on the balance, and buy ourselves a flat or maybe a house in London. How about that? We can rent it to pay off the mortgage. Well?"

"Well what? Do you think you can buy a house in London overnight? And if we're there a few months, what do we live on? Wattakka?"

But he could tell she was warming to the idea, so he wrote off to Ernie Tagg. "Dear Ernie," he wrote, "Will you give me my old job back for six months?" Ernie was a carpenter Frankie had worked for back in the old days in London, in the Eighties. In those days, Frankie's friends went around with safety-pins in their noses and purple hair. They dropped acid and went round the world on five pounds a day. Frankie did none of these. Instead, he checked out of Oxford halfway through his maths degree and became an apprentice carpenter under Ernie. Ernie made him sharpen saws and cut endless strips of moulding in the mitre-box and mark out risers and treads for staircases. But mostly, he had to unload the three-by-twos when they were delivered on site and hump about sheets of plasterboard all over the place. It kept him lean and fit.

Frankie never ceased to marvel at this strangely impermanent style of Western building where the walls went up almost by magic, and the staircases were put together by slotting risers and treads into the strings, using just wedges and glue but no nails. There was a divine poetry in all this, though Ernie never seemed to think much of it. He thought even less of Frankie's work. He replied Frankie's letter on a scrap of exercise book, written with an HB pencil.

"Dear Frankie," he wrote, "I have a client who is never satisfied with whatever I do and is very bad about paying. I think it's high time I sent you in, so she can see how *bad* bad really is. Shift your ass and get over here quick. P.S. I have the keys to a cottage in Tooting I haven't started work on, so you and the wife can kip down there."

Frankie did not show Mala the reply. She was a Minister's daughter and would not have taken kindly to the HB pencil. But he told her its contents.

"What do you think now?" he asked triumphantly.

"What do I think? I think we go consult the astrologer immediately." This was her answer to everything. If the mother-in-law had flu, if the dog had ticks, if the servants had worms, off they went to the astro.

The astro was well used to Mala's family, having been a favourite of the Minister when he was still alive. In the old days when Frankie and Mala were newly married, the Minister used to arrive in a screech of Pajeros, with motorcycle outriders, their stick arms in oversize white gloves waving away the riff-raff, like so many voodoo dolls. But the Minister had committed the final outrage by dying on them all and his family were now slowly sinking into oblivion.

Not that they realised it: they continued to occupy a colonial villa set in a vast acreage in the heart of Colombo in Havelock Town, and they continued to behave like the good little junior ministers they felt they were. Frankie's mother-in-law, the great She-Minister, had positively blossomed after her husband's death, with a severe case of what Frankie called MWS or Merry Widow Syndrome. In the old days she would walk two steps behind, smiling prettily in her silk sari, accepting garlands that were bestowed on her husband and promptly off-loaded onto her. Nowadays there were no functions to attend, no schools to open, no outriders. Nothing is so sorry as the household of a dead ex-minister. But the family spared themselves too much pain by carrying on as if nothing much had changed.

Frankie observed all this dispassionately. He was a happy-go-lucky soul to whom it really did not matter one way or the other. Besides, Mala was the one member of the family who did not behave like this. She had been too young at the time to be poisoned by the fruits of ministerial fame.

Every day Frankie's mother-in-law had a cane bucket chair brought out and placed in the center of the drive, exactly midway between the gates which were fifty yards up and the servants quarters which were fifty yards down. On this she sat in her polyester nightgown, commanding, cajoling and crowing, in a shrill voice that cried out to the four corners of her domain. Life to her was a process to be undergone, endured and enjoyed: a vast feast at an open board; a journey, not a destination.

It was all a far cry from Tooting. The house they were lent by Ernie was in one of a criss-cross of eight streets called the Tollerton Estate. Each house was tiny, about the size of their back kitchen at home, but exquisite. Not that anyone else in the area seemed to think so: the English, Frankie thought, were the most spoilt race on earth when it came to houses, in spite of having probably the best housing stock in the world.

Tooting was real Ernie Tagg country.

"Tooting should be called Tweeting, because it's cheep, cheep, cheep!" he used to sing. Frankie knew it well from having worked on so many of Ernie's sites. It was the perfect place for them, he thought, among the Tamil newsagents and Filipina domestics and redneck taxi drivers. Life was lived outdoors on the pavement, there being little room inside once the television and furry three-piece suite had taken up residence. Anytime of day or night vast women sat in the open doorways of these houses, thighs splayed apart to catch the cooling breezes, all really quite reminiscent of the she-minister back in Havelock Town.

When Mala and Frankie had got married the Minister accorded them the signal honour of the front room in the family house. It was a mixed blessing. Unusual for a colonial villa the house had no verandah, but a long series of reception rooms down the centre, separated by columned arches. On either side of these public rooms ran the bedrooms, each one leading into the next and each one appropriated by a different member of the family. Frankie and Mala's room being at the front was like Fort railway station in the rush hour. Privacy was a concept that did not exist: any time of day or night there were mango sellers, fish women and lavatory coolies knocking at their window, and screaming kids running through the room; and of course the odd postman. Both Frankie and Mala were too good-natured to resist the invasion and in any case, being the youngest, had no say in the matter.

Most curious of all, the door from each bedroom into the hall was kept open day and night with only a curtain for cover. In the early days Frankie had tried closing their door but Mala had promptly reopened it, aghast at such a sacrilegious act. Sex was therefore an unsatisfactory affair, performed in the dead of night, in dead silence, because you never knew where the she-minister might be patrolling. It was all part of the Eastern system of control and appropriation, Frankie reflected philosophically. The old controlled the young, the educated the uneducated, and as for the rich, well the rich had no doubt at all that they actually *owned* the poor.

Once, in London, when Frankie was on the bus going home from work, his saw and chisels in a plastic bag, an old Indian man sat next to him.

"You carpenter?" he asked. Frankie nodded. "You come home with me then, fix my shelves." The Indian had a surprisingly strong grip for an old man and would not let go of Frankie's arm. Frankie had quite a struggle getting off the bus at Tooting.

When he told Ernie the next day, Ernie cackled. "He had other plans for you, me old son!" Ernie had a dirty mind. But Frankie knew that it was the old Eastern concept of ownership. He was younger, poorer, and obviously working class. (Good heavens, carrying a saw on the bus!) The old man felt he had a right to own him, have him at his beck and call for an hour or so.

Ernie's current job was in Clapham, a twenty minute bus ride up the road from Tooting. For Frankie, the most delicious moment of the day was the early morning kiss and cuddle in the double sleeping bag he shared with Mala, before he headed off in the chill to Ernie's difficult client. This client was an exquisitely beautiful Ethiopian who only got up at noon and did not like to be disturbed by noise till then. The workman had to pad about silently, with even their radio turned down low.

"How do you manage to do any work?" Frankie asked. Ernie threw up his hands. Yet when she did get up she was charm itself, frying them sausages and making endless cups of strong tea. She was difficult about money too and gave them hell if they made a mess, but no worker can resist that heady combination of tea, beauty and sausages, and Ernie was loath to walk off the site.

The first thing Frankie did when he got in to work that morning was to go through the local advertiser. There were dozens of agents listed for Tooting. Ernie did not like you using the clients' phone so he had to be quick and discreet. On the fourth call he struck gold.

"We have a cottage on the Tollerton Estate within your range," said the agent, "but you have to be quick. The last one to come on the market went in twenty four hours."

"When can I see it?"

"The owner is there now. But give me all your details first." Frankie spelt out his name. There was a silence at the other end.

"You don't know me," said the agent, "but I know you. Were you a friend of Olivia's?"

Back then Frankie had been putting it about quite a bit. Olivia had been a long and particularly painful episode in his past history. "That was all ages ago," he said. The agent, whose name was Dave, called the vendor on the other line and arranged for Frankie to view the cottage straightaway.

"What's become of Olivia now?" he asked as he was about to hang up. "Does she still live in Ilminster Gardens?"

"Yes she does," was the reply. "And I live there with her."

Without telling anyone on site, Frankie slipped out and headed off to Tooting. Mala had gone to the West End for the day, to root about the shops. The house was on the next road to where they lived and easily the ugliest, having been ruthlessly modernised in the émigré style: aluminium windows, pebble-dashing, coloured cement roof tiles and a jazzy concrete grill for a garden wall. The vendor's name was Potente Militante Aguacaliente. She opened the door promptly with a welcoming smile full of gold teeth.

"Oh, Pranseez! Can I call you Pranseez?"

"Of course you can."

"And my name is..." here she took a deep breath.

"I know," said Frankie quickly.

"...But you can call me O-ping." It was the sound a cash register makes, and truly, when he looked in her eyes, he could see dollar signs.

"As you can see," she said leading the way in, "this berry good house, berry large, berry modern." Long experience had taught him not to argue. There was a velvet avocado suite on a furry maroon carpet.

"I make the garden clear," she said leading him out the back. There was not a leaf, a plant or flower: it was entirely paved over. But the house was clean and warm. Frankie thought to himself, this is it. He could picture Mala and himself making out on the furry carpet, in front of the fake log fire.

"Come, sit, I make you coffee." She sat him down at the kitchen table.

They began the delicate Asian process of haggling. She invoked pride, he invoked pity. She flattered, he flattered. She spoke of the weather, he spoke of the Gods.

"Eh Pranseez, you rich Sri Lankan people, you come here and buy everything up!"

"Eh, Oping, you live here twenty years, you richer than all of us, richer than the English even!"

She told him her life history in six easy sentences, he told her his in five. She ran down the English, he ran down the English.

It got dark. They were both exhausted. Mala must be home by now, he thought, as he staggered out, promising to come back the next day.

"Pranseez, I like you. I keep the house for you. But you pay me good price, eh?"

"Oping, you killing me!"

She cackled with motherly satisfaction as she watched him go.

Mala was at home, fiddling with the cooker. She could not cook to save her life but then back home you didn't have to. There was always food laid out on the kitchen verandah on a yellow formica table, under bright plastic covers to keep off the flies. This abundance of food more than anything else had endeared the she-minister to Frankie: he adored his food. One of the benefits of extended family life was that you never really had to do anything for yourself. There were always the servants, the aged aunts, the hangers on: the secondary characters in the play. You, as principal, just had to be, to exist. When Frankie had first come back to Sri Lanka, he had been full of the fire of go-getting Western idealism, the mantra of *becoming, becoming, becoming*. But the East has its ways of dealing with people like that. It chips away at your rock-solid resolutions with infinite patience and before you know it you are wallowing in the pleasure of just *being, being, being*. Put like that, the she-minister had her life down to a fine art; and so did the denizens of Tooting for that matter. Their pleasures were simple: the burger and chips, the cans of beer on the front doorstep, the endless tinkering with cars that never went anywhere. Their only gospel was the Book of Council Benefits. Two generations of joblessness had bred into them what the East had taken a thousand years to research and refine: that most elusive of scientific particles, the Hopeless Gene.

Mala came out of the kitchen with a double bottle of wine from Somerfields, two glasses and a single plate which contained what looked like shrivelled sheep's penises on a bed of cotton wool.

"Sausages and mash," she said briefly.

They ripped off their clothes, snuggled into the sleeping bag and watched "Who wants to be a millionaire?" while popping sheep's bits into each other's mouths. Pure, perfect happiness.

Next day negotiations were resumed. Frankie showed Mala the house from afar but would not allow her to come in till the deal was finalised.

"Eh Pranseez!"

"Eh Oping!" Today they were both a little more battle-scarred, a little more world-weary. She gave him sugar biscuits and a powdered orange drink that scoured the enamel off his teeth.

"Pranseez, don't ask me to reduce any more, please! But I leave you the small bed upstairs, ok, and the curtains." The bed was no earthly use, a small cot for the child Mala and Frankie did not have.

He offered her a thousand less than she was now asking, they were that close.

She threw in the washing machine.

He threw in a compliment.

The deal was done.

Things went quickly from there.

He retained Peter Scholl on the legal side and Ernie fixed him up with a cut-rate mortgage. Every day they went to visit Oping. She had come over from the Philippines twenty years before to be a nurse at St. George's Hospital. She was retired now. She loved the house. She did not really want to move. There was a daughter and grandson living in Crawley.

"Creepy," murmured Frankie, and Mala giggled.

"I don't go back to the Philippines now," Oping was saying, "I find it berry, berry hot. And my relations, they all ask for money. They think I berry berry rich."

"But you are, Oping, you are," Smiles all round. She was a generous woman. In the weeks before completion she promised them virtually everything in the house, the Hoover, the television, the tables, the chairs.

Frankie thought back with a smile to their visit to the astrologer, the deciding factor as far as Mala had been concerned. The astrologer was a Tamil lady, living in bourgeois splendour in Mount Lavinia. She was much in demand, especially during elections, and it was said that governments were made or broken on the strength of her predictions. There was a queue and they had to wait: a change from the ministerial days when they were given precedence at whatever time of day or night they arrived, rushed in and rushed out through the back entrance to avoid the hungry gaze of the riff-raff.

There was a large green fridge in the living room; and an indoor garden which consisted of a space ten feet by eight, with cement rocks and a waterfall, now thankfully turned off, and plastic flowers artfully placed here and there.

The astro looked critically at Frankie's shorts and skinny tee shirt and rubber slippers. She could see it betrayed a deep lack of respect for her profession. She spread out the little rolls of parchment that were their horoscopes on the table. She did Frankie first.

"You will go abroad."

She must say this to everyone, he thought, because virtually everyone in Sri Lanka prefers to live abroad.

"You are very good with your hands." (Mala giggled.) "I see you in an artistic sort of job, may be as a gardener? Or working in a garage?" Gee thanks, thought Frankie. She did not mention carpentry.

To Mala she said, "I don't see you living here at all." Mala wriggled excitedly. "What are you doing here? You shouldn't be here even now." But no consultation is ever complete without a little *frisson* of excitement, and being the good showman that she was, the astro kept it to the last.

"I see a long curved knife, like a sickle," she said. "I see a big black man."

છ   છ   છ

When the day came for them to move in they discovered that Oping had stripped the place bare. The removals van was loaded up with the chairs, the table, the washing machine. Frankie felt it indelicate to ask her why: those things were hers to give, hers to take away. Oping herself was quite off-hand with them. She pointed to two black bags in the front yard as she hurried off.

"Clothes," she said. "Berry berry useful."

What mattered was that they were in. Hand in hand they explored. The cot was gone but the curtains were there, and the lampshades. They had fun with the black bags. There were polka-dotted bandanas and glittering sequined tops and dresses split to the thigh.

"She must have been quite a girl in her day," Mala murmured. The second black bag contained a silky black cashmere coat for Frankie.

There was just one surprise: upstairs, on top of the fitted cupboard in Oping's bedroom was a curved black iron sickle.

The phone rang.

"Hi it's me, Dave, just checking that the completion went O.K. Did you get your keys?"

"Yes, thanks."

"Mrs. Aguacaliente was insisting that she bring them in here, to the Agency. I told her to hand them over to you directly, since she knew you so well, but she seemed strangely unwilling. Anyway it all obviously went off all right. And on another point... since our business dealings are now over, fancy meeting up for a drink?"

Frankie hesitated for a second. "Yes, why not?"

"Great. How about tomorrow evening, say at the Windmill, six-ish?"

"Looking forward to it." Frankie put the phone down wondering what that was all about. When he told Mala she absolutely refused to go with him.

"Look, this Olivia person is someone from your past life. I have positively no desire to meet her or anyone remotely connected to her." So that was that.

They had brought over the little black and white TV from Ernie's house, and they settled down to "Who wants to be a Millionaire?" with fish and chips and a double bottle of Algerian benzine.

After work next day, having had a furtive wash in the Ethiopian's downstairs marble loo - Ernie would have gone spare if he knew - Frankie walked up Elms Road to Clapham Common. Although it was already October the weather was surprisingly mild and there were people on the grass flying kites, drinking beer and just generally being English. Narrowly avoiding assassination by a mad mohican on a motorised scooter, he went into the Windmill. They had agreed to meet at the bar. A man came up to him.

Frankie looked with shock. The man was younger than he, no more than thirty.

"Hi, we meet at last, I'm Dave." They shook hands. The second shock was that he was Asian. They looked each other up and down and burst out laughing. They did not really look alike but there was a certain indefinable quality about both that each recognised in the other.

"Olivia's taste in men hasn't changed much over the years," said Frankie with a grin. "I was about your age when I was with her."

"Yes, I know. I've heard all about you. She never stops talking about you in fact." They took their drinks to a corner. The pub was almost deserted because everyone was outside.

"Olivia not coming then?"

Dave looked at him speculatively. "She doesn't know you're here. I haven't told her."

"Oh?"

"It took her a long time to get her life back after you walked out. I didn't think it fair to throw her back into confusion again."

"How is she?"

"Well you know she was operated on for the aneurysm?"

Frankie nodded, remembering. Olivia with her blond head shaved, her eyes smudged with black, her sister looking accusingly at Frankie, saying nothing: it was the last time he had seen her.

"She came back to the Estate Agency job after that. That's when we met in fact. But she never really settled in. She kept forgetting things. Finally she quit."

"And now?"

"Now she works part time for Wandsworth Council. Now she has me." His chest swelled out a little when he said this and you could see the pride in his young eyes. "I love her," he said simply.

Frankie's heart went out to him. The dividing line between love and pity was almost invisible. He had crossed it himself many a time. It was not something you could point out to other people.

"What made you walk out?" Dave asked.

Frankie thought for a minute before replying. "I had just hit thirty. I said to myself, I'll go back home, get married, have kids, do the decent thing." He smiled. "For me you see, it was never enough being here. I never really felt I belonged. All this running about after unattainable goals. Over here they drum into you that *nothing* is ever enough. At home you learn that *anything* is enough, you're bloody lucky to have anything at all!"

"It's different for me," said Dave. "I'm a second generation Asian. This is home. I wouldn't know what to do if I went to India."

"What about marriage? Don't your parents want you to marry a nice Indian girl?"

His eyes gave a dangerous flash. "Of course they do. Well they can sod off. *They* chose to live here. They were the ones who encouraged me to call myself Dave instead of Dev which is my real name. They'll now have to put up with a son who behaves like an Englishman."

Frankie didn't pursue it any further. He was right in what he said after all.

"And what about you?" Dave asked. "Are you happy? Did you make the right choice?"

Frankie thought of the she-minister, the open door, the screaming kids.

"Yes," he said laughing, "though it's no picnic I can assure you."

"But no kids, of course."

"How did you know?"

"Because," said Dave wickedly, "you would have been pulling out your wallet by now and showing me pictures. So why no kids?"

"Nothing quite works out the way you want it. You see my wife Mala - she is a good bit younger than me - she wants to enjoy life a little bit. We've sort of decided that we'll have kids when she gets to thirty or so." Yet another example, he thought, of the abdication of responsibility that the East encourages in its children in order to control them better.

"Biological clock and all that," Dave was murmuring. "There's fourteen years between me and Olivia. Kids are more or less out of the question for us. We're very, very happy as we are. Being older she's very understanding, lets me do anything I want. And you know, I can talk to her about work - she was many years in the business herself after all. It's thanks to her I've gone so far up the ladder so quickly. And she keeps me on my toes: an Asian girl would have been sitting at home, making me curries, fattening me up."

Frankie thought of Mala's cookery. "Don't be too sure," he smiled.

"Anyway what I really wanted to ask you is, are you here for good now?"

Was there a slight note of worry in his voice? Frankie put him out of his misery.

"God, no. We're out of here as soon as we get a tenant for the place. My life is back in Sri Lanka, however bad the war or the political situation."

What he didn't say was, he wanted to make his mark, leave his name, achieve immortality: it was easier to manage out East.

In the West they encouraged a who-wants-to-be-a-millionaire sort of life, where you doubled and doubled again your successes with lightning speed. A life of the present: and when you were past it, nobody wanted to know, least of all your children who were by then thoroughly westernized. There were many victims of this, people of his parent's generation who, having returned home too late, were condemned to wander the streets of Colombo in their weird returnee clothes, in the desolation of their dying years, abandoned by the West, ignored by the East. The secret was to come home early, before the thread was broken.

In the East on the other hand you achieved appallingly little, usually under very trying circumstances, but what you did was for ever. It was usually enough just to be, to exist, and what little you did build, stick by stick, stone by stone, was merely added to the efforts of the twenty generations before you: the long view. This is why, thought Frankie, it is so tragic when an easterner leaves home. However successful he is in the new country, he has in one easy stroke wiped out the efforts of countless generations before him. No amount of polyurethane varnish can ever replace true lacquerwork.

You could not expect Dave who had grown up in the West to understand all this. It was something he had only come to realise himself after twenty years away.

Dave looked at his watch.

"Jesus, it's late! I'd better get back. She must be wondering where I've got to."

He was not as free a man as he imagined. Frankie watched him go:

"There, but for the grace of God," he thought.

❧ ❧ ❧

When he got home that night Oping was there. "She was actually in the house when I got back," Mala whispered to him in the kitchen.

"Eh Pranseez! Just thought I'd visit, see how you getting on. I had another key, you see. I leave it for you now when I go."

"I caught her removing the lampshades," muttered Mala. "She would have taken the bog-roll next."

"Pranseez, I came to warn you. Don't give my mail to anyone else, right? If they call for me, don't tell them where I've gone."

"But Oping, we couldn't even if we wanted to! You never even told *us* where you were moving to."

"Yes," she said cryptically. Mala and Frankie had found it curious that she was so evasive whenever they tried to ask. They knew it was somewhere close, but that was all.

Smoke was pouring out of the kitchen. Mala appeared with plates. "Swedish meat balls," she explained. "Oping won't you stay to dinner?"

Oping sprang to her feet with the agility of a mountain goat. "I have dinner at home," she said hurriedly. She looked at the plates.

"These Swedes, they have black balls, eh?" Cackling, she went away.

❧ ❧ ❧

The days got shorter. The Ethiopian's work was nearly finished. Oping took to coming every evening, always under cover of darkness, in her furry hat and coat: a game old grenadier in drag.

"Eh, Pranseez," she would whisper hoarsely through the letterbox, "Is that you?"

"No, it's not," he would whisper, opening the door. She would chat awhile, collect her mail and go. No mention was ever made of the stuff she promised and then took away. She never stayed to dinner.

On weekends the Tooting toughs came out on the streets, all dressed up and nowhere to go. They raced their cars up and down the streets. Later on in the evening, when the beer had taken effect, the fights began. Curled up in their sleeping bag, Frankie and Mala would listen. It was better than anything on TV.

"Bastard! Slag!" Every week the same life histories, the same biological details. Then, to round off the evening, there were egg fights. It brought back fond memories of Havelock Town.

The calls from the she-minister were getting more frequent. "When are you coming back? You must understand it is very difficult for me here, I have to manage on my own..."

"We'll have to get back," they said, cuddling each other, "but not just yet, not just yet."

Then one freezing Sunday morning, when Frankie padded down in his cashmere coat to bring the milk in, he found an enormous black man at the door.

"I apologize for troubling you," he said. "My name is Winston. I've been waiting here since five in the morning when I came off my shift. I didn't want to wake you up."

Frankie didn't want to let him in, even though he was so polite and well-spoken.

"I am married to Mrs. Aguacaliente's daughter." Bit by bit the story came out.

"Guadalupe only married me for my money. From the first day, man, she was taking and taking." He had bought her gold chains and clothes, the television and the washing machine. Frankie began to feel uneasy.

"In fact I bought most of the things in there," the man said, pointing inside the house. It was all becoming clear. Oping had been very free and generous with other people's stuff.

"When the baby came along, it was me who spent. I worked double shift, day and night, night and day. She was a nurse too, like her mother, so she was earning good money, man. But what was mine was hers, and what was hers was hers too, you know?" He was breathing heavily. His accent became more West Indian.

"Everything in this house, man I bought with me own money. She not interested in culture and all that thing, man, like you other Asians. She only want money. Is her mother I blame, is her mother.

Two months ago, she made me move to Crawley, because she said it easy to get work there in the hospital. One day I come from work and they gone, man, they gone."

It had all been beautifully planned, Frankie realised. Oping's daughter had moved into rental accommodation as far away from Tooting as possible, so Oping could sell up without her son-in-law's knowledge. Why? Frankie wondered. Did they owe him money from the sale? The day Oping moved, the daughter and the baby must have disappeared from Crawley and moved back in with her.

Perhaps there were other, darker reasons for Oping's daughter to want to escape with the baby. Frankie thought of the iron sickle upstairs.

Don't even go there, he said to himself, it's none of your business. The irony was that they were probably somewhere close by, maybe even on the next street.

"I don't know where they went," Frankie said truthfully, "and they took everything with them." Then he relented a little. "If you like, I'll give you the agents' and the solicitors' addresses." He wrote the details on a scrap of paper and handed it to Winston.

Winston still did not go. He kept shifting from foot to foot, looking hard at him.

Frankie said, "This is yours, too, right?" He unbuttoned the coat and handed it over. He began to shiver because he was only wearing his shorts underneath.

"What will you do if you find them?" he asked.

"I'll kill them," said Winston simply.

Two days later, all hell broke loose. When he got back from work, Mala said, "Peter Scholl's been trying to get you all day. He tried to speak to me, but I said he'd better talk to you." Even as she spoke, the phone rang. It was Peter Scholl.

"Mr. Bandara," he said, "you sent a Mr. Winston here, did you not?"

"Yes, why, what did he do?"

"Oh nothing much. He only tried to break the door down. Then he threatened my secretary, then he threw my mobile out of the window. I had quite a job pacifying him. He left me and went off to tackle the agent."

"Mr. Scholl, I'm really, really sorry."

"Well all right. Just don't do it again."

Frankie put the phone down and it rang again. It was Dave. Dave was more succinct.

"Bastard," he said and hung up.

Then the phone rang yet again.

"Pranseez, did you tell him where we lived?"

"Oping, I don't *know* where you live," he answered wearily. He wanted to add, if I did, you wouldn't be alive now. "By the way, we are leaving on Friday."

"Yes," she whispered hoarsely, but he could tell she did not believe him.

ରେ   ରେ   ରେ

The new tenants were moving in at the weekend and Dave was going to let them in. It was odd, Frankie thought, that this house which had seen possibly the happiest months of his life, had been the scene of so much misery to others. He would leave them to their Afro-Asian wars: he was going home to Sri Lanka, to continue the patient process of building, stick by stick, stone by stone. He locked the door and popped the key through the letterbox. As he handed Mala tenderly into the minicab that was to take them to the airport, he thought with a slightly sinking heart, of the mango sellers, the screaming kids, the open door.

The Window Seat

When he saw the little Regency window seat next to Surangani's laundry basket, Kapila's pulse quickened a little. It wasn't exactly love at first sight. More like lust.

"As you know, I have this close relationship with Jesus," Surangani was saying. What fun for you, he nearly replied, but stopped himself in time. Instead he let his mind dwell on the little cane stool with its reeded legs that would look so well against the one long window in his warehouse.

Kapila bought and sold old furniture, and was that rarest of beings, the unmarried Sri Lankan male who didn't live with his mother. In fact his mother had never forgiven him for moving out at the age of twenty, to a little piece of land left by his grandfather, where he literally camped out in a cadjan hut till the warehouse was built.

"What will the neighbours say?" she had wailed. Even now, years later, she skilfully avoided any mention of his profession when friends asked, dwelling rather on the luminous medical career of her younger son.

"Kapila?" she would say airily, "Kapila is just waiting for the right girl to come along, and after he gets married, *then* he will start this *big* import export business…"

"Are you paying attention?" Surangani interrupted his reverie.

"Yes, yes of course. You want me to get rid of the bed and the wardrobe to make room for your…" here he hesitated before he used her phrase "…your Prayer Clinic."

"Yes please, sell them at any price. There just isn't room for them in here. It's so wonderful, Kapila," she continued, "when Jesus speaks to Enid, it fills us with this light… We feel so honoured, and it all happens right here in this very room… And Enid is his *vessel*…"

Years before Kapila had had this thing going with Surangani. Surangani with the lustrous eyes and the body to die for. Surangani whose darkly aboriginal good looks got her nowhere in a country where a woman is nothing if she's not Fat and Fair.

Back then it wasn't Jesus that kept her going, but the astrologers. Every week they would go to Mr. Silva in

Katana, Mr. Perera in Imbulgoda, Mr. Fernando in Panadura. Came the day when one of them said, "I see this big silver bird and your prince is stepping out of it." (Kapila had just returned from a visit to an aunt in Australia). Next week another said, "I see the slipper and it fits your foot." (What sort of fairy tales did these people read, anyway?)

But Kapila panicked: he decided it was time for him and Surangani to part company. However, the two of them remained good friends. In fact Surangani was his only female friend. His male friends, all of whom were single or divorced or just plain unmarriageable claimed it was impossible to have a woman as just a friend. Kapila disagreed, but they pitied him anyway, because Surangani didn't fit their perfect ideal of womanhood, which was also for the most part derived from fairy tales...

Kapila looked at the wardrobe. It was solid and heavily carved, with a lacy fretwork pediment: a deeply unfashionable Victorian matron in a frilly starched cap. The double bed was slightly better, a satinwood reproduction campaign bed.

"I'll see what I can do about these," he said. "By the way, what will you sleep on when the bed goes?" It wasn't the sort of question you normally asked a girl like Surangani, but after all, he knew her well enough.

"Oh, I'm moving in the single bed from the spare room. Arul can sleep on that. The floor is *quite* good enough for me."

"But is that *quite* good enough for Arul?"

She didn't seem to know what he was getting at, so he dropped the subject.

In the intervening years after they had split up, Surangani had met and married Arul, a big bear of a man who had the patience to put up with her every whim. After the astrologers there had been the Year of the Dog, when she went around rescuing everything on four legs and her flat in Slave Island began to look like Canine Central. Kapila wondered at what point Jesus had crept in, but it looked like He was there to stay...

❨ ❨ ❨

When Kapila got back home, Selvam who minded the shop during the day had locked up and gone home. The warehouse looked bleak and forbidding in the thin green evening light. It was the worst thing about living alone, coming back to an empty house. Some days he went round the rooms switching on the lights one by one, whispering to himself, my God, my God, why have you forsaken me?

Kapila had built the warehouse as simply as possible, eight concrete columns supporting a tin roof. His friends called it minimalist and his enemies called it cheap. Up the middle of this space rose a dramatic staircase which Kapila had designed out of old H-irons and discarded hardwood railway sleepers, with a rope for a handrail. This led to a sleeping platform which overlooked the shop area. He couldn't really imagine a woman sharing these quarters with him, but the nights were lonely. It was difficult, after all, to curl up in bed with a bombé commode. And sometimes, when the monsoon rains beat incessantly on the tin roof, and his mind was filled with melancholy, he would long for something dark and aboriginal to come creeping up the rope staircase, though nothing ever did.

(((

Next day Kapila went back with Mudalali to collect Surangani's furniture. Mudalali was a man of few words, his vocabulary consisting mostly of hawking and spitting. Kapila could not afford a lorry of his own so he hired Mudalali for his removals and deliveries. When they got to Surangani's they could hear the strains of an aged seraphina floating down from the flat above, and chanting. Kapila remembered that the people upstairs were devotees of Swami Chinmaya.

Mudalali and he lifted the pediment off the wardrobe and began to dismantle the sides.

Then a thought struck him.

"Doesn't this belong to Arul?" he asked Surangani.

"It used to be his grandmother's. But he fully agrees with me that it's got to go. There just isn't enough room in here when my people (*my people*) come to worship. And Enid needs lots of space. Some nights the room is overflowing with worshippers."

The chanting from upstairs was getting louder.

"And how do you manage with them?" he asked, pointing up at the ceiling.

"Oh, I've told Jesus, you handle it, it's your problem."

Then a slightly malicious glint came into her eyes. "Anyway help is on its way. I've sent Arul to fetch Enid. You know she sings like an angel. She also plays the tambourine. Tonight's our weekly Wednesday session. You'll stay of course? 6.30 to 8.30 prayers and singing, 8.30 to 9.30 clinic time, when people ask questions and Enid answers. You know, the other night Jesus spoke to her on the way here from Battaramulla, and Arul had to pull the car over and wait till He finished. We had to delay the service over half an hour till they got here!"

Just then Arul walked in, stopping dead in his tracks when he saw the dismantled wardrobe. He opened his mouth to speak and shut it again.

"And this is my Enid," said Surangani triumphantly.

If Kapila had been expecting a woman in homespun cotton sari and pigtails he was in for a rude shock. Enid wore flowing flared pants and a well-filled halter-neck top. She was Fat and Fair. It was easy to see how she could pack a room full of devotees. She stepped forward and put her arms around Surangani and Arul.

"I am *so* lucky to have found these lovely people," she said. "If I have been able to help others with my gifts, it is only because of the help and generosity of these two. I only pray to Jesus to grant me a lovely husband just like the one Surangani has found in Arul."

Arul looked distinctly embarrassed. Kapila silently loaded up everything onto the lorry.

Then he went back inside to make his excuses to Surangani for not staying on.

"Well I won't keep you, you cynical old dog," she said. "But remember the miracle of prayer. If there's anything you need, just make a request and Enid will pray for you. You'll be surprised how soon your wish is granted."

"By the way," he said, "you know that stool you have in the bathroom, next to the laundry basket? Do you want me to sell that too?"

"That old thing? You can have it. I only ever use it to put my feet on when I clip my toenails."

((((

Back home Kapila got to work. He got out his little black book and started calling round his small circle of buyers. These were mostly rich young couples who were in the process of constructing their various houses. They usually relied on Kapila to find them the right object for the right room. If they bought, Surangani was in luck. They never haggled and they always paid cash. If none of them were interested the pieces might remain in the warehouse for months, if not years.

Of course the warehouse also contained items that were not for sale because they were too rare, or simply because Kapila had taken a fancy to them: the ebony salon suite from the Soysa Walauwa, for instance, or Gajaman Nona's painted cabinet. Kapila had placed the window seat under the long window at one end of the warehouse. He knew that it too was a piece he would never part with.

The satinwood bed went almost immediately, but nobody wanted the wardrobe: it was variously too wide, too high, too frilly. Surangani called him daily, supposedly to get a progress report on the sales, but in fact to tell him all about the latest developments at the prayer clinic.

"You won't believe how nice the room looks now, Kapila, without all that furniture. We've put mats down on the floor. Enid of course sits on the small bed because unfortunately she has a rheumatic knee."

"Unfortunately."

"And the miracles! So far, we've cured cases of peritonitis, asthma, bleeding piles…"

"Bleeding hell!"

"Shut up!"

"Do you think Enid can do anything about premature ejaculation?"

"Don't be disgusting!"

◖◖◖

Weeks passed and the wardrobe wouldn't budge. Kapila came back one day to find Selvam in a state.

"There's a gentleman in there who's not a buyer or seller. I don't know what he wants, but he says he needs to see you."

Kapila went in to find Arul perched on a Soysa Walauwa chair. He was balancing on its hind legs, gently swinging back and forth. A thin film of sweat broke out on Kapila's forehead.

"Hey Arul, my man! Come over *here* and tell me what's up!" But Arul didn't get up. He just gently continued to rock, back and forth, back and forth. Any second now Kapila expected to hear the ebony crack.

"I've come to ask you a favour," Arul said, "in strictest confidence." His eyes looked unhappy. "I've come to ask you not to sell the wardrobe."

"Well there it is," Kapila pointed out.

"You know it belonged to my grandmother?" Kapila nodded. "I know it's big and bulky, and I know Surangani needs the room, but…"

He looked at Kapila helplessly.

"Look, if you don't want the wardrobe sold I won't sell it, and I won't tell Surangani either. I'll give Selvam instructions - any time she decides to have it back you just come along and collect it, whether I'm here or not. By the way," he continued, "how are the prayer sessions going?"

"Enid is just wonderful! But I worry that it's all getting a little out of hand. Last Wednesday we had thirty people squeezed in there. And old Mrs. Wadugodapitiya started speaking in tongues."

"I always knew she had a dirty mouth."

"And now Surangani has introduced music. Enid brings her family over. Her mother plays the violin, and her brother the tabla. They're very poor and Surangani has taken them all under her wing."

Kapila was silent. He had always been a believer, but for him true faith came from a single spark, blazing forth from the mind to the wide open universe beyond. You couldn't ignite it to order every Wednesday evening between 6.30 and 9.00 in somebody's back bedroom. He had no faith in these group sessions anyway, which smacked of self-indulgence. *Ah me, look what a sinner I am, but aren't I just wonderful to admit my sins to y'all?* Maybe the fault was his, he thought, being the way he was. For him religion was a one-on-one thing: the loneliness of the long-distance runner, not the all-boys-together heartiness of the rugger buggers.

"How are the people upstairs taking all this?" he asked.

Arul grinned. "It's a competition. You know how Surangani is. When they sing loud, she sings louder. But there've been one or two ugly incidents, when our people's cars have blocked theirs, and vice versa. Trouble is, Surangani's such a child. I think she's absolutely loving all this."

Kapila remembered only too well. That was one of the things he had loved about her. She was a child let loose in the Sistine Chapel with a red felt-tip pen, trying to join the hands of Man and God with a dotted line.

Arul got up to go. "I only pray it won't all end in tears," he said.

As soon as he was gone Kapila seized the chair he had been sitting on and examined it minutely for cracks. But the chair held good and true. Silently he sent up a prayer of thanksgiving to the carpenter of Moratuwa who had made it.

((C

Weeks passed and the phone calls from Surangani stopped. Kapila went back to his normal daily routine. He kept his word about the wardrobe - it was an easy piece not to sell. With the peace process advancing, the Jaffna market was opening up, and he and Mudalali made several trips up north in the lorry, to check out the few remaining Dutch houses up there. It was during one of those trips that Mudalali said: "You know that couple who drove in while we were dismantling the wardrobe? I've bumped into them several times at the kadé close to my house. Last time I saw them they asked for my number. Said they might have a job for me."

Kapila was not quite clear who he meant, and the Mudalali never brought up the subject again.

The following Wednesday evening they returned from Jaffna with a good haul of blue-green antique windows. While they were unloading the phone rang.

"Hi Kapila! Just calling to find out the status of the wardrobe."

"It isn't sold," he answered truthfully.

Surangani launched into a long spiel about her devotees. Her voice was high, almost hysterical, and Kapila wondered for a moment whether she was about to start speaking in tongues. He listened silently. In the background he could hear the low murmur of the crowd, like waves breaking on a distant shore.

"We have almost fifty people here tonight," she was saying. "Arul's collecting Enid on his way home . . . God, those people upstairs are getting on my nerves. They've just begun their chanting. They do it on purpose, you know. They are always trying to upstage us. I can't *think* what's keeping Enid. Maybe Jesus is speaking to her ..."

It wasn't Jesus that was keeping her, Kapila knew. It was Arul. He and Enid had come that morning in Kapila's absence and taken the wardrobe away.

"...I don't know *what* I'll do if they don't get here soon."

"Maybe you could speak to the crowd yourself," Kapila suggested, "you may be a vessel too."

"You know what? I might just do that. They're my people too, after all. And I've always prayed that I could be of some service to them."

Suddenly, absurdly, he asked, "Shall I come over too?" But she didn't answer. She had her people - the great comforting roar of the ocean - behind her and she certainly did not need him.

Silently Kapila put the phone down.

Be careful what you pray for, he thought, because you never know, you might just get it.

Surangani had got her people and Arul had got his wardrobe. And Enid had got her Arul. As for Kapila, he'd got his beloved window seat, and damn useful it was too for cutting his toenails on.

Love

Max Kohlmeyer lived in a cosy flat above the Cornmarket. It was clean and neat and terribly nice, from the bare polished floorboards to the Stanley Spencer prints on the walls. A bay plant in a black lacquered pot stood discreetly by the kitchen door. Max hated trendiness of any sort. Had he realised that Stanley Spencer was a current Oxford trend the pictures would certainly have had to go.

High above the university streets, Max led a charmed existence. Every day after lectures he brought home from the market round the corner some tempting treat - a rabbit perhaps or a plump rainbow trout - which he would lovingly prepare and approvingly consume. If Max was aware that other students lived almost exclusively on a diet of fish and chips and brown ale he never showed it. Food was the one great passion in Max's life.

The other was Arabella. Arabella was an orange tabby cat more familiarly known as Puss, but there was a strict understanding between them that she should never be referred to by that name in public. Arabella was dozing in the sunlight contemplating the evening's menu when the door opened and Max staggered in with several brown paper bags.

"Hiya Puss," he said, dumping them on the dining table. "I bought us an eel today." Arabella wrinkled her nose appreciatively and leapt lightly onto the table. "Also two pigeons. I thought they'd be nice stuffed, one for you, one for me." There was a purr. Every good cat knows her pigeons. Their conversation was interrupted by the telephone. Max picked up the receiver wondering who it could be.

"Max Kohlmeyer here." There was a pause.

A hesitant female voice asked, "Is that Max Kohlmeyer?"

Marvelling at such powers of feminine intuition, he waited.

"It *is* Max, isn't it? It's Marion here," the voice continued breathily. "Oh Max I hope you're not in a bad mood. It's just that... Do you think we could ask you a great favour? It's such beautiful weather, and Harry and I were thinking..." (Max's eyebrows crept up in surprise) "...we were thinking how lovely Oxford would be with all those spires and things, and wouldn't it be lovely to spend the weekend there. Oh Max can we? Are you there?"

Max took a deep breath. "I could think of nothing nicer, Marion. You needn't have asked. You know you're always welcome, both of you!"

"Oh you're such a darling. Expect us around four-thirty this afternoon, O.K?"

"Come a bit earlier, I've got a tutorial at five," but the receiver had gone dead already, and Max hung it up with distaste.

Only then did it occur to him that it was still only Wednesday. Never mind. How could you put out such sparkling enthusiasm? Marion and her boyfriend were close-by, at Reading University, an hour away in their little Sprite. An hour too close, Max sometimes felt, but such sentiments were always replaced by feelings of guilt. He began to feel guilty now. The two of them had the freshness and simplicity that only love could breed. Theirs was a love with a capital L. Effete Oxford society shuddered and shunned love as being something ghastly and redbrick, but Max in his simple way had long ago shunned Oxford society. He himself was now in that uncertain no-man's-land, *Waiting for Love*, as the song goes. There was no point going out to look for it because a gentleman never does. Max sincerely believed that one fine day it would arrive at his doorstep all neatly parcelled, with a 'sign here for receipt of delivery' note pinned to it's elegant back. In the meantime there was Arabella to share the bed.

Marion and Harry blew in at half-past four that afternoon, thirsting for a cup of tea.

"Don't get up, I'll make it," she said, disappearing into the kitchen. He heard her dropping the kettle.

"And how are you, old boy?" Harry asked in his slow, leisurely way. Harry was large and tweedy. He smoked a pipe.

"Not too bad, not too bad." Max tried to keep his mind off the sounds in the kitchen. Max had been at school with Harry, but even that had not prepared him for Marion. But Love had to be forgiven its crimes, he thought. They talked about old acquaintances, one of whom was giving a party that night to which Marion and Harry were going. Max had given up such outings a long time ago. He couldn't endure the shrieks and screams of the smart set without feeling weak at the knees and sick in the pit of his stomach. Only love could pose unhurt in such a setting because by it's very nature it was turned in on itself and could escape the pawings and scratchings all around.

The tea arrived, surprisingly in one piece. "Now don't you bother about dinner. I'm going to make you something smashing before we go. And don't you wait up for us either," Marion instructed him. Max got up to go for his tutorial. The eel would have to wait. More's the pity, he thought, but Love did not survive on such delicate fare, and it was unfair to put it to the test.

After the tutorial Max strolled back lightheartedly to the flat. Spring had not yet arrived, but the shop-girls flirted willfully under the yellow lamps of the Cornmarket. God was in his heaven and there was a good film on the box. A large note was propped up on the mantel at the flat: "Your dinner's in the oven. Enjoy. See you tomorrow." 'Your dinner' turned out to be a large wicked-looking hamburger. Max swept it into the dustbin regretfully and sighed, for Love must be forgiven its crimes, but there were levels to which even Arabella would not stoop. He dined on a lightly boiled egg and afterwards took the sleeping-bag out of the hall cupboard, for it was unthinkable that Love should not have the only bed in the house. Arabella was not quite of the same opinion, but she was used to sleeping in the sitting room with her master when Marion and Harry were in town.

Max slept the sleep of the innocent and his dreams were peopled by postmen knocking on every door with large gift-wrapped parcels of every shape and size. It must have been in the early hours of the morning that he was woken by the sounds of stiletto-heels passing dangerously close to his head. Max lay very still.

"He looks like a cuddly baby, doesn't he?" Marion whispered loudly. She giggled tipsily and lurched off towards the bedroom with Harry.

"Harry?"

"Hm?" Max could hear their voices through the bedroom door.

"Has he ever been in love do you think?"

"Doubt it." Max could hear more giggles, and scuffling.

"Harry? I've changed my mind." Marion's voice had the absolute finality of one who has drunk too much. "He's not a cuddly baby. He's an old woman." Max closed his eyes and two fat tears rolled silently down his cheeks...

Marion and Harry woke up late next morning. After a long bath they sat down to a leisurely breakfast. There was an enormous note on the table. "Gone for lectures. Am having lunch in College but dinner's on me, so do be back on time if you go out. Max."

What a dear he was, Marion thought. It was extraordinarily kind of him to give them the run of the place whenever they came up. The sunlight turned everything in the flat to gold, and as she lay back in her chair smoking, it seemed to her that Oxford had never looked more beautiful. She would go for a walk with Harry in Christ Church Meadow. But first the breakfast things, for Marion was a good soul and always did her bit. She stubbed out her cigarette on a saucer - there did not seem to be any ashtrays about - and took the dishes into the kitchen. When she was emptying the cigarette butts into the bin she noticed her hamburger nestling coyly in the refuse. She forgot all about the washing up...

Max returned to the flat in the afternoon to find stale cigarette smoke in the air and cold dishes in the sink. He did not care. There was a strange glint in his eye and Arabella, who had got up to rub herself against his leg, thought better of it and stayed where she was. With lightning quickness Max opened all the windows and did the dishes. He opened the fridge and took the eel out. For the next few hours he busied himself in the kitchen. Arabella had never seen such purpose of mind in him before. It was almost as if he were in love...

When the pigeons were in the oven and the eel was simmering on a slow fire, Max came out of the kitchen, poured himself a stiff gin and tonic, and settled down with a book. That is how Marion and Harry found him when they came back in the evening. Their day had not been a success. There had been a lot of nasty smelly cows in the meadow and Marion had accidentally stepped in a cow-pat. It had been cold down by the river and to cap it all, their lunchtime salad had been stale.

"And so, darling Max," she concluded, "We are both starving. What have you got for dinner?" And without waiting for an answer she went off to the kitchen to have a look. She opened the door and the hot fumes of garlic enveloped her. Max could hear her coughing. One clove the recipe had called for, but Max in his wisdom had put in twenty-one. There was a shriek and Marion came rushing out of the kitchen and fell into Harry's arms.

"There's a snake in your pot!"

"Snake?" Max opened his eyes wide in surprise. "Oh, you mean the eel."

He laughed. "Have you never had it before? One of my favourite dishes, eels in wine and garlic, and P... I mean Arabella loves the head of course."

"Of course." But Marion didn't sound too sure.

When they sat down to dinner Max opened a bottle of white wine.

"To celebrate Love," he said holding up his glass and looking through it at them.

"To Love," they echoed uncertainly. The eel arrived, resplendent on a china platter, and after much coaxing Marion was persuaded to have a piece.

"Wonderful," she said, but she sounded worried. Max chatted amiably. They were showing 'Casablanca' on television that night and he was looking forward to it. When they had finished with the eel he brought in the next course.

'A kiss is just a kiss,' he croaked, putting it down on the table.

"What," said Marion with all the dignity she could muster, "is that?"

"Pigeons, stuffed with chocolate," Max announced triumphantly. "I picked them up at a little shop off Trafalgar Square when I was down in London." Marion smiled, but her smile looked sickly. She stared at Harry, and then at the pigeons which Max was busy carving up.

"Harry?" she asked uncertainly, "Isn't it Joyce's birthday today?" Her voice gained confidence. "Aren't we supposed to be at her party tonight? My God, we're supposed to be in Reading tonight." She sounded hysterical. "Quick," her chair scraped back, "if we leave now we can be there in less than an hour." She disappeared into the bedroom and reappeared with their overnight case. "Come on Harry what are you waiting for? Max, I'm sorry, but we *have* to be in Reading tonight. How silly of me to have forgotten."

Harry got up awkwardly from his chair. "Goodbye old boy," he said sticking out his hand. "Sorry about all this. We'll see you some other time."

Max listened to the clatter of the stiletto heels on the staircase. He remained motionless for a long time, until it was very faint. Then he poured himself a glass of wine, slowly. He raised the glass and fixed his victorious eye on Arabella.

"Here's looking at you kid!" he growled.

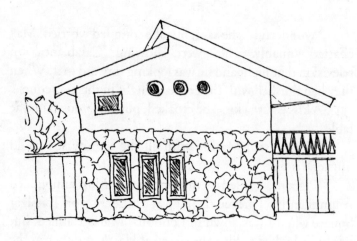

Pack Up The Moon

The old man died as he had lived, with no trouble to anyone, slipping away quietly on a Sunday afternoon.

I had just walked back home to my yellow rice and chicken curry when they called, and I could tell they were annoyed that I had left them at the crucial moment.

"It's happened. What are we going to do?"

"I'll be there in a second," I said, but I took my time. You know me, my yellow rice and I are parted with difficulty. For me, the old man had died a long time back, at least a month before. I had watched him as he made his sure-footed way down, circle below circle, as his body, and then his mind left him, and the slow sweet smell of corruption set in.

By the time his children arrived from England his mind was all but gone, and when they walked in through the door a big foolish grin lit up his face, like a strong light in an empty room. How could I tell them that the doctors were killing him with their many kindnesses and their strong pills?

I had been through many crises with him in the past ten years, fought in bleak hospital rooms with no one else around and he had survived them all, because he was a tough old Kandyan from the mountains. But he was also of a generation that believed implicitly in the power of Western medicine, and relished that little brass tray of pills that was offered up to him daily. Once, when he was really down, he had said to me in the depths of his despair, "It's all been such a mess, hasn't it?" He was crying, and I had to hold his head in my arms.

"Of course not," I had lied.

And who was I in all this, you might ask. Me, I was just a friend from two streets away, who fed him and washed him, and carried him to the bathroom like a baby, and tried to make him go by turning on all the taps. I remember very well the last time he communicated with me. I had just finished giving him his lunch and his Kandyan relations walked in, big square-shaped people in their old-fashioned jeeps and their dusty limousines. I got up to go because there is only so much a good neighbour can take. The old man gave me a look of panic but I was unrelenting, and as I left him his face softened and he gave my hand a slight squeeze. For me that was his last goodbye. After that there was only a rusting hull, settling slowly to the bottom of a murky sea.

I won't bore you with the sordid details of death, the shit on the bed sheets, the wicked catheters, the bedsores like wounded strawberries, and always and everywhere that slow sweet smell of death, like tea with too much milk in it.

Have you ever been present at a Sri Lankan death? No? Well I can tell you that the body is barely cold when the fun begins. People come from far and wide. Your neighbours, who have hitherto never been allowed past your front door, finally get a chance to inspect that damp patch on your back bedroom ceiling which you never had time to do anything about. And they will examine very thoroughly, because they know they'll never get another chance. They will check the tins in your kitchen cupboards and the softness of your guest towels. And all the while they will weep copious tears while being fed and watered at your expense.

The old man in his wisdom had decreed a cremation, unusual for a Catholic. I was dispatched to get the Death Certificate. I went from the Cinnamon Gardens police to the Colpetty police, to a woman in an upstairs room next door, who threw open her windows dramatically and directed me to Ward Place. (Was she a Registrar? I shall never know.) I came to an iron staircase again leading to an upper room. There was a man seated on the bottom step. He shook his head when I asked him for the Registrar.

"He's out! You'll have to come back at six."

"But he's meant to be on call all the time!"

"Don't ask me," he said, "I have nothing to do with it!"

At this moment the Registrar himself decided to intervene. A disembodied voice from upstairs floated down.

"I'm not here," it said, "Go away! Come back at six if you need me." So what to do until six? I went off to Seram's, where all the smart people go to get buried. They were very nice to me in those marble halls. There was a motto in bronze lettering over the door. I think it said "Dying to serve you" but I couldn't be sure. They took me upstairs and showed me the coffins.

"The basic job costs 45,000," they said, "and that includes the embalming, the vase and the two candles."

"Never mind the candles," I said. "He has to be cremated, and the sooner the better." They were a little unhappy at this, but cheered up when it was found that the crematorium was fully booked for the next day and so it had to be the day after.

I chose a coffin that was neither the cheapest nor the most expensive. By the time I got back it was night and the house was thick with neighbours. There was a pride of nuns huddled over the body. I tell you there was more praying done there that night than in all the game parks of Kenya. I left them to it and walked home.

The cremation was short and sharp and there were not many people: just the basic hard core, in at the kill, so to speak. The old man had outlived all his friends and indeed his enemies. I am proud of the fact that I did not cry, not even when they asked me to press the little green button to start the fire, thinking by mistake that I was the head of the family.

Did I grieve for him, you ask, did I grieve? Well, let me tell you that I grieved all the time, every day, till that final month. Most of all I grieved as I ran round the park, in the sodium yellow hours of early morning. And I grieved as I did my sit-ups on the wet grass, while the sun rose lazily over the jacarandas. But in the last month that grief turned to mechanical weariness, when it took two hours to feed him a quarter cup of coffee, and another two for a quarter glass of water. Life dripping away by the teaspoonful.

There *were* the odd moments of hope. Once when he was really bad the priest was called in, a tall man with a rum-rich voice and a Portuguese name. And halfway through the last rites the old man sat up, and a sigh escaped his lips as if he was singing. But he was gone again the next day, back into his coma. It had just been a blip on the screen.

The funeral festivities were endless: the seventh day dhana, the one month almsgiving, the memorial mass; and always he was present, that slow sweet smell. At every step the guests ate their fill with much grief and gusto.

It was after the mass, I think, that they decided to open the will, which the eldest boy produced. I was the only outsider there, having stayed behind to tidy up. The old man hadn't much to leave, a lifetime of fair success followed by a series of bad investments towards the end. They all got pretty much what they expected and deserved.

"Listen to this," said the eldest, who was reading it out. "To Ashoka my friend, I leave my *kavichiya*." I held my breath. The kavichiya was not his most valuable possession, but easily his most valued. It was an ebony couch, a severely elegant thing with Grecian lines on which the old man used to take his afternoon naps.

There was silence in the room.

"But you wouldn't want it, would you, Ashoka." It was a statement, not a question, so I didn't bother to reply.

I put away the last plate. The old man was gone. It was time for me to go too.

As you can imagine I didn't bother to say goodbye.

◈   ◈   ◈

It must have been a good three months later that the doorbell rang, and when I opened the gate, the familiar blue van drove in. It was Chuti, the youngest and in many ways best of the bunch.

"I have your kavichiya," he said. "It wasn't easy to extract, as you can imagine." Together we unloaded it in the front yard.

"I won't take it in if you don't mind, my back's playing up. In fact, I'd best be getting along. I wouldn't want them to think we were getting too friendly!"

The van drove off.

There was a wind blowing in the yard and it was getting dark. As I stood there, he was there with me, that slow sweet smell. Three seconds, four seconds, and he was gone, but the kavichiya remained, glowing and resplendent among the shabby palms.

Eternity

Is it possible to behold eternity in a single night? Can you not feel the strength, the infinite patience of the train as it creaks its way out of the village station?

And those school children talking outside your window, are they not moving too, in long loose-limbed strides so that they are still outside your window, still casual and casually still? Beings from another world who you have the good fortune to observe for a moment, before they board your world unnoticed and become part of you, your quest for eternity.

And as you travel down the coast with the gilt-edged sea on the one hand and the crumbling pink palaces on the other, do you not feel a sense of communion with your fellow passengers? That street-child for instance, with the voice as harsh and sweet as the mint humbugs she is selling, does she not have the face of a girl you once loved?

And every once in a while the brilliant light of the setting sun is reflected in the cracked window of a sugar pink façade, and you drag yourself reluctantly after your eye to view the dim dusk of nonexistence within. But only for a moment and you are back outside again, shivering in the safety of the salt air, unspeakably thankful that you are you and they are they.

And now it is dark and one of your fellow passengers, an old man, squats on the floor of the carriage and begins to blow a reedy instrument. The caustic dissonance of his sound is only the music of eternity because it carves out of the air crude images of unspeakable beauty, a glimpse merely of what lies beyond. You listen in the darkness in fear and longing for this is what you have been looking for all your life.

And now it seems as if you are travelling over the sea which is of a blackness such as you have never seen before. Its roar has the strength, the infinite patience of eternity. And every once in a while it throws up from below out of the pure generosity of its heart a crushed handful of black ice, through the open door-way of your carriage.

Is it possible, you ask yourself, is it possible?

And you have to answer, *Yes! Yes, a thousand times is it, possible!*

For you saw it only yourself the other night.

Acknowledgements

My heartfelt thanks to Kamini de Soysa if not for whose vicious and persistent bullying, this manuscript would still be lying at the bottom of the Jackwood almirah, and to Sarojini Sinnathamby who bravely knocked it into shape on her machine.

Also to Sam Perera and Ameena Hussein for having faith in me.